# BRAMWELL

# BRAMWELL

## RUTH GATHERGOOD

*Bramwell*

Copyright © 2019 by Ruth Gathergood. All rights reserved.

No part of this publication may be reproduced, stored in a retrieval system or transmitted in any way by any means, electronic, mechanical, photocopy, recording or otherwise without the prior permission of the author except as provided by USA copyright law.

This novel is a work of fiction. Names, descriptions, entities, and incidents included in the story are products of the author's imagination. Any resemblance to actual persons, events, and entities is entirely coincidental.

The opinions expressed by the author are not necessarily those of URLink Print and Media.

1603 Capitol Ave., Suite 310 Cheyenne, Wyoming USA 82001
1-888-980-6523 | admin@urlinkpublishing.com

URLink Print and Media is committed to excellence in the publishing industry.

Book design copyright © 2019 by URLink Print and Media. All rights reserved.

Published in the United States of America

ISBN 978-1-64367-200-7 (Paperback)
ISBN 978-1-64367-199-4 (Digital)

Fiction/Horror
08.01.19

My family home was a little cottage which stood alone at the end of Wodolf road, right next to where an old church stood. The church was over two hundred years old, held a lot of history and had been neglected over time to become its' present ruins. The stone built had dilapidated to a big heap of rubble, spiting efforts of fine architectural men who built it. Great history lay within its haggard walls and as a result, it became the village monument. Seeing old pictures of it, was disheartening and echoed sorrows of its' past beauty.

    I lived in the cottage with my mother, father and two sisters, Charlotte and Sophia. Sophia was a couple of years older than me and Charlotte three years younger. My name is Suzanna Thomson and I am twenty years old, this is a story of my family and the ghostly encounters which we experienced at Bramwell cottage. We had lived in that cottage for just over a year having moved from a little flat in Somersby after my dad gained a small fortune from his father, a wealthy cattle ranch owner. The ghostly experiences started happening a few weeks after moving in the cottage. Charlotte came tumbling down the stairs one night petrified and screaming, her face looked pale as if she had seen a ghost. Her whole body was shaking like a leaf, begging for someone to listen to what she had to say. That night my parents and I were sat in the lounge, celebrating new years eve, while Sophia was out with her friends. Charlotte however had decided to go to bed early as she was not bothered about celebrating new years anymore, of which was understandable.

"New years are always the same and I don't know why people keep exonerating them, as far as I know it is just another day," she had said.

That night she was claiming to have seen a ghost of some old woman in her bedroom, and that the old woman was trying to communicate with her.

"She grabbed my hand," Charlotte exclaimed.

"Her hand felt cold and clammy, and she was pointing at the fire place in my room. She looked about eighty years old, short in stature, with grey hair. Her eyes were big and round like two big mulberries, and sea blue in colour, she looked nervous and kept pointing at the fire place."

"What woman?, just calm down," said dad.

"I hope you are not thinking it is a ghost Charlotte. I am sure it is just a figure of your imagination, or maybe you were dreaming," he added.

Mum and I looked at each other without uttering a single word, at the same time being bemused, then she shook her head.

"It is not one of your imaginations Charlotte, is it? because you are always full of them," she said.

"Mum! I know exactly what I saw, it was a ghost of a ghastly woman in red," she panted.

"In fact, I can still see her horrible dirty fingers covered in coal fire soot, oh God! it was terrifying, why don't you believe me?"

Dad took a sigh, before reassuring Charlotte.

"I am sure it is nothing, though I remember old Jimmie from the village liquor store mentioning something like, 'the old cottage being haunted'. Old Jimmie is a veteran of the village, he has lived here all his life. He told me of a tragedy that befell a family that once lived here, he said one day the cottage just went in flames and killed the whole family, a family of six children including the mother and father."

"That's quiet some story," mum said.

"To think that happened here, it is eeiry, mm it is giving me goosebumps," she added.

"I have always suspected that there is something weird about this village, what secrets do they hide," mum said. A few times I have been to the grocery shops, the locals have kind of stared at me funny and whispered to one another, what they were talking about, I don't know, there must be something about this cottage that they know of and are unwilling to share with us, I guess old Jimmie's story can verify that," mum added.

While the conversation carried on, I seemed completely disinterested and simply huggled myself around the open fire. The fire place was my favourite place to curl up around every evening, especially the wintry days.

"Nothing like a glorious blazing fire in winter," dad always said.

Last winter I spent one entire day by the fire cosy, and ended up spending the entire night in the lounge, till Sophia woke me up in the morning with her loudness. Anyway, after the discussions of old Jimmie's story, Charlotte decided to calm her nerves by having a shot of straight whisky, before heading back to bed, while my parents and I stayed up till Sophia returned home from her night out. After her return, we all decided to go to bed without informing her of Charlotte's story.

# CHAPTER 1

Early next morning, being our Sunday ritual Charlotte and I went to the grocery store to buy some fresh bread and bacon from the local butchery.

"What do you think of the ghostly figure that I saw in my room last night?" Charlotte asked me.

"Do you think it was real? perhaps we should dig from the locals about the history of Bramcote cottage, I am sure somebody is bound to know something, especially the older ones who have lived here all their lives," she added.

Charlotte and I had always got on well, we were very close to a point of doing everything together, as well as confiding in each other. She was my best friend, it was different with Sophia. Sophia was a working girl, ambitious and had her own circle of friends. She was a lot more outgoing unlike me and Charlotte. Sophia worked as a clerk at the local municipality. Charlotte and I were a little on the quieter side and enjoyed spending a lot of time at home. Dad once said, it was depressing for him to see Charlotte and I waste our lives roaming around the house doing very little. He spoke of trying to marry us off to some hard working men and hopefully that they will inspire us to do something with our lives. That was unfair of dad, because neither Charlotte and I wanted to marry. We wanted to spend the rest of our lives together. mum disagreed with dad, she said she wanted us to be ourselves, after all she was as close to her sister in a similar way. She said she never dreamt of marrying neither, till she met dad, who simply swept her feet away from her sister.

"I couldn't agree with you more," I told Charlotte. "Perhaps we should dig, especially if we bump into old Jimmie, he seems to know a lot about this village more than anybody else," I added as we trod along the high street, walking in a similar pattern, as if mirroring each other. As Charlotte and I were talking we got interrupted by a voice calling from behind us.

It was Ms Biggs a widow who lived by the creek facing Almer primary school, the one and only primary school in the village. Ms Biggs' husband had died two years prior from lung cancer. Rumours had it that, he was a chain smoker, he had started smoking a lot after being laid off work at the local Quarry site, where he had worked for many years as a labourer.

"Suzanna! Charlotte! wait up," shouted Ms Biggs. "How are you girls? and how is your mother?. I haven't seen your mother in weeks, she hasn't been turning up at the women's club. Is she is alright?"

Charlotte and I smiled, then Charlotte replied,

"Oh we are fine Ms Biggs and mum is alright, she has just been so busy of late. She got a few chicks, you see, for the cottage, and is planning on rearing them for eggs. It has been keeping her quiet busy," Charlotte continued.

"I totally understand," Ms Biggs replied, "I wish I could have the energy your mum has, I could do with having a few chickens myself, but having the two dogs and a cat keeps me busy enough," she added.

For me running into Ms Biggs became a perfect opportunity to dig a little about the history of Bramwell cottage, I scratched Charlotte's arm as if to say shall I ask? In response, Charlotte secretly scratched my arm and nodded her head in agreement.

"Ms Biggs", I asked.

"Charlotte and I are researching about the history of our cottage, is there anything that you know, since you have literally spent your life here."

Ms Biggs looked at me funny, while rubbing her chin. "Why do you want to know girls?" she asked.

"Some things are better left unsaid," she replied nervously.

Charlotte winked at me, then said, "Oh! don't fret Ms Biggs, we are just curious especially the cottage being so old, it must have some stories, we thought."

Ms Biggs looked around nervously as if to see whether anybody was listening to our conversation. She rubbed her chin again nervously before replying.

"I don't know whether I should be telling you this girls, a long time ago back in the fifty's, a fire broke out at the cottage killing a whole family, six children including the mum and dad. Nobody knew how the fire started and who caused it. Rumours have it that, there was a police cover up and the locals gagged from ever talking about it. If anybody spoke of it they were terrorised and threatened and eventually forced out of the village."

Ms Biggs coughed excitedly as she spoke and at the same time nervously looking around to see if anybody was listening. "Ms Biggs," I said excitedly, "please do not worry, it's only that my sister here Charlotte saw a ghost of a ghastly old woman in her bedroom, and she was trying to tell her something. So we thought you might know something about the cottage, which our family do not know anything about."

Charlotte immediately grew frightened and at the same time appeared well composed, she simply grinned without saying a word.

"I have heard some stuff," Ms Biggs continued, "but I shouldn't say because I don't want end up banished from the village like the others."

"What others? Ms Biggs, "if there is something, perhaps you should tell us, just in case our lives could be in danger," I exclaimed.

Ms Biggs appeared more terrified, and then said, "Sorry girls I cannot tell you anymore, I am afraid." "And please girls you haven't heard anything from me, she cried before disappearing briskly into the crowd.

Charlotte and I looked at each other again, in a perplexed manner, each of us lost in thought of what it was Ms Biggs was scared to reveal.

"That was something," Charlotte exclaimed as we bustled in the busy street.

"I know, I wish she had told us more," I replied.

"I hope we bump into old Jimmie, he is bound to know more," I continued.

After our shopping, Charlotte and I decided to sit in the local park for a while and digest what we had just heard from widow Biggs. It was a beautiful day, the sun shone with its majestic glory, revealing its innocence, purity and simplicity, as compared to the corrupted humans beneath.' The innocence of nature,' I thought to myself. Here we were Charlotte and I trying to unravel a horrid mystery, and yet nature being so beautiful. We sat in the park next to a lake swarming with birds of all colours, there was a few ducks nesting right in the centre of the lake where there was a little isle. Everything in the park was in season, the grass was luscious green, shimmering lavishly. 'How wonderful it is when the flowers blossom and the trees too. The beautiful scent permuting, that attracts the butterflies of many kinds and birds of all sizes,' I thought to myself. I gazed in the park, I was amazed, for a minute I was silent and stuck in time and stuck in paradise, those few minutes lasted forever, drawing me away from the puzzle Charlotte and I were trying to put together.

"I think we ought to find out more Suzanna," Charlotte said. She startled me as my mind was drifting away. "Yes of course I replied in awe, please let's do." Before then we gathered our shopping and headed straight for home.

When Charlotte and I got home, vicar Simms was there, the local church vicar. Him and dad were sat in the kitchen, chatting away while smoking his pipe as usual. Sophia was in the drawing room playing Mozart on the piano, while mum was in the garden tending to her chickens. We greeted vicar Simms and after, we put our grocery away, Charlotte and I decided to go to her bedroom to search for any sign or clues that might have been left behind. And who was the old lady, that Charlotte saw in her room, I was curious because I wanted to see her too, so I could be convinced of Charlotte's story. We both got excitable and decided to pull off the carpets in her bedroom. Underneath lay a Packard wooden floor, besides that, there was nothing mysterious at all, we searched to see if there was any loose tiles, hoping to find something buried beneath. But there was nothing, the floor was as smooth as a whistle, we looked at the fire place, and decided to leave it till last. We searched and searched and eventually we saw an air vent near the window, it looked haggard and dusty.

"This might be it," Charlotte said excitedly, "go get a screw driver, I bet you there is something in there," she added while grinning away.

I went to the kitchen to get the screwdriver, dad and vicar Simms were still chatting away. "Everything okay here, I suppose?" the vicar asked dad.

"I heard from Ms Biggs down in the village, that something was off here, that is one of the reasons I dropped by, besides my weekly visit here for a cup of tea," the vicar continued.

"Everything is fine, yeah," dad replied while scratching his head, he was debating whether or not to tell the vicar of Charlotte's ghost story.

"Everything alright, Suzanna! the vicar shouted as I quickly ran back upstairs to Charlotte with the screwdriver, the vicar had glared at me in a terrifying manner while I was in the kitchen searching for the screwdriver, it send shivers down my spine.

"Did he know something about the hauntings at the cottage?"

It crossed my mind that the only reason he came to visit was to find out whether we knew anything about the cottage's secrets.

"So did you get it, I mean the screwdriver?" Charlotte asked.

"Yeah I did, I got more than a screwdriver, I got the strangest glare from vicar Simms," I replied.

"It seems like he knows what we are doing, he must know something, no doubt," I added, while handing the screwdriver to Charlotte who by then was ready and waiting standing on an old chair so that she could reach the air vent.

The minute Charlotte unscrewed the vent, a swam of flies came shooting out of the vent, almost blinding Charlotte that she fell off the old chair, injuring her left foot. Lucky enough, it was not a serious injury. Charlotte and I were in awe, it was very creepy indeed, dad heard the racket and shouted from downstairs,

"Are you okay girls, up there!" he yelled. "We are fine dad," I immediately replied.

The last thing I needed was dad coming up and messing up our little escapade. I was determined to find something mysterious in that bedroom on that day.

"Do you think, that was some sort of evil sign?" Charlotte asked nervously.

"I believe so, who knows," I replied while nodding my head.

I immediately opened the bedroom window, and the flies flew out, there must have been hundreds of them, big black flies. I had never seen flies that big before, even Charlotte agreed with me. Charlotte and I took a breather before pursuing on our mission. I offered to climb on that old chair again to look inside of the air vent. I reached my hand inside, it was quite a long vent, my hand stretched right through the air vent till eventually, I felt something metal. I pulled it out, it was very light. It was an old black key with an inscription SAC.

"Look what I found Charlotte," I exclaimed, "I knew, we would find something," I continued.

Charlotte's eyes glistened, "What do you think it's for? it must be some form of a clue," she added. Immediately another swam of flies came shooting out of the air vent again, that is when Charlotte and I screamed, then ran out of her room, it was a bad omen.

After we gathered ourselves together, we went back to her room, the flies were gone, we had no idea where they disappeared to.

"Perhaps we should look, up the chimney," Charlotte suggested.

"Remember that is the place the old lady 'ghost' was pointing at."

I scratched my head for a while, I began to think the whole thing was becoming preposterous "Charlotte, I think we have gone too far with this thing," I said.

I took a sigh, "Are you sure about what you saw? I mean the ghost. I would like to see it for myself so I can believe you Charlotte," I added.

"We could get a Ouija board if you like," she replied. "I know where we can get one from, there is a pagan shop in town, you know, at the back of Masons super-market, next to the book shop, you know. The shop is open all day, 9am to 5pm, every Monday to Monday, they don't get many customers you know, that is why they are open everyday. I hear it is a family business, run by some pagans who used to be gypsies," Charlotte replied excitedly.

"Why not hey, let's go for it," I replied.

"Just promise we will use it when mother and father are out. You know every last weekend of the month, they go off to auntie Doris', in Cornvalel, it will be perfect time. You know what this means, persuading Sophia to join us in our little mystery hunt," I added.

"How about the chimney? that is where you claim to have seen the ghost, I will look up myself," I said to Charlotte.

I wanted personal experience myself, or encounters as you might call them.

"Of cause," Charlotte, replied hesitantly," be careful though. If you see anything, always know, you are not alone, I am here," she reassured.

I quickly dashed to the fire place with a broom, I thought to myself if I can't see anything, I was willing to go as further as poking the chimney funnel itself to see if there was anything up there. I searched around, and did not see nor hear anything, so I pocked the chimney funnel with the broom. The more I did it, the more black soot came raining on me like a cloud of dirt.

"Keep at it," shouted Charlotte, as my eyes and ears kept being distracted by the heavy snow of soot falling on me. I fiddled once more, and down came this black crow from the chimney, with it's wings wide spread. Charlotte was disturbed by the sound, she couldn't see what it was, but I could though slightly obscured by the soot fog.

"It's a crow!" I screamed.

"What!" Charlotte replied in awe.

"A crow! come see for yourself," I replied.

"Now something seems to be making sense," I added.

Before I could remove my head from the chimney funnel I heard a faint cry, it sounded like,

"Help us please! please help us."

It sounded like two female voices accompanied by children's voices. Before I started doubting my senses, and reacting quickly to escape the funnel nemesis, I bumped my head hard on the chimney beam, and passed out.

"Are you alright?" that was Charlotte's voice, waking me up.

Vicar Simms was holding my head up. And I, all I heard him say in an echoey manner was, "What you girls been up to? I hope you are not waking up the dead."

Dad was trying to force a glass of water on me, I galloped few sips down before opening my eyes and gaining awareness of what had just happened. My eyes laboured to open, I kept hearing vicar Simms voice, murmuring something about awakening old ghosts. Dad poured the rest of the water on my face and before long, I was fully recovered. Charlotte held my hand and whispered in my ear, "Don't say a word Suzanna." I got up and I felt fine, and thanked vicar Simms for helping.

"Accidents do happen all the time, especially in old houses," vicar Simms said to dad.

"Anyway, she seems fine, I ought to be going anyway, sermons call, and that has got to be done," he said before reaching out for the door, and dad behind him.

"What about your cup of tea? Dad shouted, "You barely touched it," he continued.

"It is fine Ed, I got carried away with our conversations and I simply forgot, perhaps next time. Tell your wife, I will be staying for dinner next time I drop by."

"You haven't heard of a 'Father Francis, have you? Well never mind," he said as he proceeded to the front door.

Dad politely followed him behind, "That is fine vicar, the door is always open," dad replied before bidding him farewell.

Charlotte and I quickly got back to our escapades, "Shall we tell mum and dad of our discoveries," Charlotte asked. "I think we should wait till we find out more," she added.

I took a pause, before replying, "If they know what we have been up to, they will put a stop to it instantly, so definitely a bad idea, how ever we should try and convince Sophia, if we are going to use the Ouija board while they are away."

# CHAPTER 2

Charlotte and I decided to burn the crow, on the fire place, of cause, and nobody would ever know of it. I went downstairs and got barbecue fuel, and we set the crow on fire in Charlotte's room, soon after, Charlotte and I felt a gush of air, moving from her room to downstairs and out through the front door, that is when vicar Simms opened the door, on his departure. It was perfect timing, when he opened the front door, the crow was completely burnt, and the spirit found it's way out. Soon after our discussion we went downstairs for supper, Charlotte and I remained quiete throughout while contemplating on what we had done and seen. Sophia was out as usual, so mum didn't serve any supper for her. She came in about midnight when everybody in the house was sound asleep, she always tip toed in the house after her nights out for fear of waking dad up, because he would go ballistic and shout at her. As we lay in our beds snoring away, we heard a loud noise, it sounded as if somebody was drilling through the walls of the cottage, the whole cottage shook as if there was an earthquake. The noise was so violent that, it woke the whole family up.

"What's that noise!" dad shouted.

Mum dashed out of her bed, her night cap looking crooked and her hair flying out like a crazy woman. Her hair was brown in colour and started greying from the fringe. It was the grey bits hanging out of the cap carelessly. The few wrinkles on her face were protruding boldly because of the fright.

"Is everybody okay?" she screamed as we all gathered downstairs in the hallway as if ready to escape through the front door. We were all there except Sophia.

"She must have slept through all that, how can one sleep through that noise?" dad said.

"Sophia! Sophia!" mum shouted.

There was no response, "I will go up there and see if she is alright," she said.

"Help! help me!" cried Sophia from her room. She whimpered in her soft voice as if lost in the middle of nowhere.

Without an utter we raced upstairs to Sophia's room. Dad couldn't open her door, it was as if it were locked from the inside.

"Try opening from the inside Sophia", he called.

"I can't, I am trying, how can it be locked when there is no lock, help me dad," she yelled.

Dad tried kicking the door in, but it was of no use.

Sophia felt helpless sobbing away.

"There is an old woman in my room! help me dad!!! how did she get in her!" Sophia screamed. She lay there on the floor with her body curled like a ball.

Immediatelyl the lights went out.

"Go grab a torch Suzanna," dad shouted,

"You know where they are, in the cupboard under the sink."

In the mean time, Sophia crumbled onto the floor, helpless like a church mouse. The old woman was getting closer and closer to her uttering something that Sophia could not understand.

"Who are you! what do you want! mourned her voice. The old lady slithered towards Sophia and whispered, "It lies within the old church, it lies within the old church."

Then she simply vanished into the smoke, which by then had masked her room. When I got the torch for dad, he immediately went to the basement, that is were all electric switches for the cottage lay. The light switch was down, so he switched it back on, and all the lights came on.

"At least that's something," he uttered to himself before dashing back upstairs to try and rescue Sophia.

Despite the lights coming back on, Sophia still couldn't open her door. She sobbed and sobbed and cried out,

"Mum! the old woman is gone, get me out of here!".

As she lay there by the door, curled up, blood started dripping down her bedroom walls, on the ceiling was an inscription which read, SAC, and right beneath, read,

'Help us, we are in trouble.'

Sophia became dumbstruck, her whole body was shaking and immediately she felt icy cold, lips and fingernails turned purple. Dad, tried and tried to force her door open, eventually, he succeeded.

"Holly! Jesus Christ! what was that?" he cried while hugging Sophia.

"Sweetheart, I am glad you are okay," he sobbed.

"Is somebody playing tricks with us."

"Dad, do you see all that blood on my walls, do you see that on my ceiling, it reads, "Help us, we are in trouble."

Dad helped Sophia up,

"I'm glad you are alright," he kept repeating himself. "I can't see no blood though sweet heart, and neither do I see any writing on the ceiling. It's all in your head, I guess you are traumatised by what has just happened.

We all are sweetheart, don't worry about it, as for the old woman, she does not exist, I think you are thinking of what Charlotte thought she saw in her room, days ago. Do not worry, these stories tend to play with people's imaginations."

Mum was standing by heaving away in panic, still with her night cap looking scewy.

"Come and have a hot drink downstairs," she insisted holding her by the hand and leading her out of her bedroom. A hot drink was beneficial for the rest of us, so we all sat down and talked about what had just happened. The fire in the lounge brought a sense of comfort. Dad then decided to go to our neighbours' cottage to find out whether they had experienced the same tremour and noise as we did.

# CHAPTER 3

Our neighbours was an old couple, in their eighties, they had always looked out for us from the day we moved in to Bramwells. The Jones had eight children and twelve grandchildren and a couple of great grandchildren who all lived away and hardly visited them, so sometimes they felt lonely and so dropped by Bramwells every now and then for a cup of tea. mum and dad adored them, and looked out for them likewise. Each time they dropped by, the sweet old couple brought cooking apples, they had a few apple trees growing in their backyard.

Dad knocked on their door gently as he did not want to frighten them, especially that late at night. Old Mr Jones came downstairs in his long Jones and was also wearing some tatty, old white vest.

"What can I do for you Ed?" he asked anxiously while pulling up his drawers.

He was breathing heavily and appeared startled, "Excuse the heavy breathing, it is only, you startled me, nobody knocks here this late. You see, Audrey has got a heart condition, any kind of unexpected noises tend to startle her. What is it, I can do for you."

Dad gathered his momentum,

"Mr Jones, sorry to wake you and Audrey up, did you happen to hear loud noises followed by a tremor? We experienced a tremor in the cottage, it tore down one side of the cottage wall, so I came to check whether you are okay," he asked.

Mr Jones scratched his bold head, where he had a few hairs growing either side of his head, forming a nice big bold circle in the middle of his head. He coughed and coughed, he sounded wheezy being a chronic asthmatic,

"Hang on Ed, I need to get my inhaler, why don't you come in, you will freeze out there.," Mr Jones responded.

Dad walked in the tiny little cottage, Mr Jones reached out for his inhaler which was on an old welsh dresser in the hallway. Audrey was beginning to stir,

"Who is it Carlos? she shouted sounding half asleep. Audrey was a sweet old lady, no more than five feet tall, she was known in the village as granny Audrey, as she was sweet to everybody in the village. She did a lot of charity work, in the small community. She had a soup kitchen for the homeless which opened every Tuesday afternoon at the town market. Being a small community, there were not many homeless people, that is why it was not so demanding of Audrey, but nevertheless, she kept faithful and loyal, and opened it every 1pm on a Tuesday without fail. She had big blue eyes, narrowly separated by a small sharp nose, her forehead slightly obscured by a bushy, grey fringe, accompanied by bushy grey eyebrows. She spoke with a slight stutter, and having to wear oversized dentures, didn't help at all. She always struggled to keep her false teeth in place, once Charlotte and I took her for a pub lunch of steak and chips, she struggled so hard with her beef because her teeth kept falling out, after having struggled to walk to that pub anyway, she dragged her left leg along which was a result of an unsuccessful hip operation. We heard that Audrey's family had tried sueing the doctor, but were unsuccessful because he had fled the country. Carlos was more of a timid guy, that he let the whole suing procedure go.

Audrey came downstairs, with a struggle, dragging her leg along,

"What is going on Carlos? Do you realise it is one in the morning," she said.

She was perplexed to see dad there,

"Are you alright Ed? what is this? waking us up, in the middle of the night," she questioned.

"You know, my heart ain't good, are you trying to give me a heart attack? I might be old, but I still have got a lot to live for, you know, she added.

Her hair was all muffled up under a night cap, revealing her forehead which she so hid from the public. Carlos gave a wink at dad before shouting back,

"It is only Ed from next door! he wants to know whether we heard loud noises or experienced a tremor, because they just have at Bramwells! I told him no! You can go back to sleep honey! nothing to worry about!"

"She gets a bit upset," Old Carlos said to dad, with a gentle smile on his face.

"Don't send him off yet Carlos!" Audrey shouted, "I want to talk to him, "she shouted again while reaching out for her walking stick as she approached dad in the hallway. "What is this I hear of an earthquake?" Audrey questioned.

She was wearing odd stockings, one blue the other orange, not even dad could miss that, her night dress was navy blue with a white inscription which read, 'greatest granny ever,' she instantaneously offered dad a cup of tea.

"It is two sugars isn't it Ed? I need to tell you something Ed, your house creeps me out. Many things have happened in that house way before you moved in," Audrey said hesitantly as she made her way to the kitchen, dragging her leg along.

She pulled down a chair and sat down while waiting for the kettle to boil,

"Sit down Ed and make yourself comfortable, I want to tell you some tales of your house, she insisted."

Dad pulled an old pine chair, which kind of matched the table and the rest of the furniture in the tiny kitchen and made himself comfortable.

"Jane was asking after you, since you haven't been round Bramwells of late," dad said calmly.

"You know Audrey, a lot of strange things have been happening at Bramwells lately, my children experiencing weird phenomenons. A few weeks ago, Charlotte claimed to have seen a ghost of some woman in her bedroom, and tonight Sophia claimed to see the same ghost in her bedroom. Her bedroom door locked by itself, we do not have any locks on any of the bedrooms in the cottage."

Dad straightened his clothings in discomfort as he spoke. He did not want to speak of it, because his tone of voice changed and he kept fidgeting.

"What is it you were going to say Audrey?" he asked while rubbing his face.

Audrey got up to make the tea, then Carlos came into the kitchen after taking a few puffs of his inhaler.

"I feel much better," Carlos said as he joined dad, and Audrey in the kitchen.

Audrey gave dad his cup of tea, and reached out to Carlos to give him his, she struggled to pull a chair out while holding her own cup of tea.

"Many years ago," she began,

"A family lived in your cottage, a man, wife, and their six children. He was a clergy man, with strong ties to the local church and community, he was of Mesopotamian descent, 'so many believed,' he was highly religious, but many in the village suspected him of delving in to satanic cults. Many believe he was not alone in the village, rumours went flying that, he was occulting with high members of society in the village. I mean powerful people, they believed that, beside being the God fearing vicar, on the side, he was a devil worshipper, alongside a few powerful men. They believe he started a different religion, of which only the chosen few became part of. Their religion, was about, money, power and control of the whole village and even beyond, he became a rich man overnight, remember Ed, I have always lived here, I mean in this cottage. My parents used to live here, and their parents, Carlos, purely married into it, when Carlos and I got married, that was forty five years ago. Back in those days, you had to do as your parents say, lest you get cast out of the family, so dad insisted that Carlos move in with us. It was a tight squeeze as you might imagine, but anyway, soon after the marriage, dad fell gravely ill, and he died, and a couple of years later, mum died as well, leaving just Carlos and I in this cottage.

We stayed in the cottage, up to present day, all our children were born here, so you see Ed, this place has got a lot of history. Audrey coughed a bit, as if in excitement, she wriggled her bottom in the chair, as if ready to continue, with her undaunted story. Her eyes wondered from dad, to Carlos, as she spoke,

"That's some story, dad exclaimed.

"I knew, there was something odd about that cottage, even though, my logical mind told me, it was obscene to harbour thoughts like that, about a beautiful home, dad insisted.

"Biscuits, anybody," Audrey persisted.

As if excitable, finally came an opportunity to express herself freely, about the mysteries of the village.

Audrey remarked, "Rumours had it that, the vicar,,,"

Carlos, interrupted Audrey, by getting up to grab some old cloth from the sink, as he had spilt his tea by accident. "Carlos I wish you wouldn't interrupt me like that, when I am in a middle of a conversation, this is important,"

she croaked.

She sipped some more of her tea, then proceeded, "Oh! it was a big mess! burning his whole family down, including himself, for some ritual practice, nobody could ever understand that, the whole family died."

"Don't some people say, these satanic rituals started way before the Adamsons, Audrey?" Carlos interrupted.

"Of cause, they do," Carlos, Audrey replied.

"The mysteries date back to the early eighteen hundreds, Ed. you see, those Abbey ruins, just next to your cottage, that is were they believe it started from. That Abbey has been there since the late seventeen hundreds, rumours have it that, then they used to practice satanic rituals, right behind them walls," Audrey continued.

A father Santos, was then the Abbey priest, and he lived in your cottage, wiith a few monks from the Abbey who lived in this cottage. Rumours have it that, despite being Christians, there were also luciferians, they say, they say they used to practised all forms of occulting, from ritual child abuse, to human sacrifice, so they gain money power, and total control of the given population," Audrey added.

Dad appeared perplexed, by it all.

"So in a way, it explains everything," dad replied sceptically. "Every inch of my body tells me that, all this is illogical." Audrey drew a long breathe, then replied,

"Believe what you want to Ed, but all I can say to you, is welcome to the other side of reality.

I believe it, and so does Carlos, but what you conclude, is all up to you."

Dad took a sigh,

"This is all too much to take in, you couldn't politely top up my cup of tea would you Audrey," he asked politely, and at the same time bemused.

"What ever you say Ed. I feel you should get your family out of that cottage, and out of this village all together, things is just going to get worse for you, please Ed, I am begging of you, do the right thing for your family," Audrey persisted.

Dad shook his head, he looked at Carlos, as if begging for his opinion.

"What shall I do Carlos?" he asked.

Carlos looked down, as if in prayer, he made the sign of the holy cross, muttered something, that was not coherent, then uttered,

"An old wife's tale always turns out to be true, so like Audrey, I urge you to take your family out of that cottage, and go. Where you go, I don't care, as long as it is out of that cursed cottage," he responded.

While Carlos was in the middle of talking, the lights started flickering and soon after the phone rang.

"I will get it, Carlos shouted. He reached out for the phone, which was hanging on the kitchen wall. Dad and Audrey remained quite, they thought it was mum, on the other line.

"Hello! hello! Carlos said.

But the line remained silent. "Hello!" Carlos said once more, but there was still silence.

"It must be Jane wondering why I am taking this long here, maybe they are facing power surge at Bramwells, that is why you can't hear her," dad responded.

The lights flickered once more, before Carlos put the phone down. Audrey got up,

"I need to show you something Ed, let me go to the library."

Audrey struggled to get up from that imprisoning chair which had left her bum completely numb, somehow it was cutting down circulation from that part of her body, she wriggled her bottom, to promote that so much needed circulation. As she reached for her walking stick, her stick went flying to the side of the kitchen, thrown by some unseen force.

"Did you see that?! my stick just went flying just like that, by itself Audrey exclaimed.

Dad and Carlos were too preoccupied that they didn't notice.

"What are you talking about, Audrey?" Carlos questioned.

"My stick, my stick! it went gone flying right across there. I think it's the entity!, it does not want me to show Ed the big black book, Carlos," Audrey gasped.

"What are you talking about, woman? what book? and what stuff?" Carlos questioned again.

Audrey Looked petrified, as if some unseen force was in her presence, trying to block every attempt to help dad. She began to stutter, and tremble in fear.

"Carlos, you know that mythology book about this village, which I showed you a few years ago, it belonged to dad, and it has remained in the library ever since."

The lights flickered again, before the electric went. "Carlos! Carlos!" Audrey shouted in the pitch dark. "I can't breath, get my angina tablets from the bedroom." "Calm down Audrey," urged dad,

"I am sure it is just a power surge, I will grab your tablets, where about are they in the bedroom?" dad questioned.

"Carlos, don't you worry, stay there, I will grab them."

Audrey was breathless, and moving her hands about to try and feel, Carlos, or dad.

"They are on the side drawers, next to the bed! I can't breathe, it is that thing Carlos! attacking me now! it doesn't want me to help Ed and his family" she shouted. She struggled for breathe, then muffled,

"If anything was to happen to me today, Ed, the book is in the library, second shelf, third on the right, mythology of Grange house village, go now Ed, and remember what I have just told you," Audrey gasped.

"Oh boy," dad whispered to himself before dashing up the stairs of that tiny little cottage, dad was worrying deeply about Audrey's health and at the same time felt guilty, for dragging this sweet old couple into our problems. He got to the bedroom in pitch darkness, and had to feel with his hands for the drawers, and when he found, he had to feel for a box of pills. He got them and came back dashing downstairs.

"I have got them Audrey!" he shouted, "Have you got a torch Carlos?" he asked.

"We need a torch, so that we can see that we are giving her the right pills."

"It is the only box of pills, that she has got, her other medications all come in liquid form, so you know, they are the right ones," Carlos responded.

"I do have a torch though, it is in the cupboard under the sink you will be able to feel it Ed," Carlos added.

Dad felt for the kitchen cupboard, and fished out the torch, he could never have missed, as it was the first thing he felt in the cupboard, thank God the batteries were still working. He shone the torch at the pills, and of cause, it read, 'glycerine nitrate, for angina only, take one tablet, and dissolve under the tongue if experiencing chest pain.' He opened the box immediately and took one tablet out.

"Here you are Audrey," shouted dad.

He shone the torch at Audrey. Audrey did not respond, her head was resting on the kitchen table, with her arms drooping down.

"Audrey! Audrey! wake up," shouted dad, but there was no response.

Carlos just stood there helpless.

"Pop the tablet under her tongue, Ed," yelled Carlos.

Dad put his head, next to Audrey's mouth to check whether she was breathing, he struggled to feel any breathe.

"She is not breathing," replied dad.

"Carlos! she is not breathing! quick, call the ambulance." Dad checked her pulse, but couldn't feel anything, so he quickly dragged her off the chair, and started resuscitating. He struggled for a good while without any hope, it was only when he was giving up, that is when he felt a pulse, and Audrey was breathing again, by then the ambulance arrived. The paramedics could see very little in the pitch dark and had to rely on Carlos torch and their own torch. They put Audrey on the stretcher, before reaching for the front door, Audrey was chocking, black foam was dripping out of her mouth, it stunk like hell. "What is that coming out of her mouth," one of the paramedics shouted. "What's going on," Carlos shouted.

He held Audrey's hand, "You're going to be alright Audrey," Carlos said, he was crying.

Audrey started shouting out,

"Those spirits are trying to kill me Ed, they don't want me to help you, you have got to get your family out of that cottage, Ed."

She wriggled, and wriggled, trying to get herself off the stretcher.

"Don't allow them to take me to the hospital Carlos, you know how I feel about hospitals Carlos, I will never come back alive Carlos," she sobbed.

"It is for the best Audrey," Carlos replied,

"it's your heart Audrey, trust these gentlemen, they will look after you, besides there is Ed, you know he cares about us, right."

"I will go with her to the hospital, Carlos," dad said persistently.

"But I will give Jane a call, and she will come spend the night here with you here, don't you worry about a thing, alright, Audrey will be fine, as long as she is far away from all this, she will recover Carlos," dad insisted.

Carlos said his good byes to Audrey as they put her in the ambulance, and dad by her side, by then mum was there with Carlos. The ambulance blue lighted all the way to St Thomas', the local hospital, it wasn't far off, from the common market in the town centre, it was a good twenty minute drive from Bramwells. Audrey was taken straight into the emergency room, and from there she was put on a cardiac ward, to monitor her heart, dad stayed by her side all the time, reassuring her, and comforting her that Carlos was going to be fine. In the mean time, mum was trying to persuade Carlos to get some sleep, she didn't even want to talk about the whole experience. She had brought a couple of old lamps from our garage, for Carlos, it was a good thing that they still had some oil in them. She lit one in Carlos and Audrey's bedroom, and the other one she kept downstairs, in the lounge, where she was going to sleep.

"Thank you Jane, thank you, very much, God bless you and your family," Carlos kept saying.

"It is okay Carlos, much appreciated," mum whined. The last thing she expected, after the happenings at Bramwells, was more happenings at Carlos' and Audrey's, and let alone, having to find herself spending the night there. She made Carlos, a nice cup of cocoa, and led him upstairs to his bedroom.

"Good night Carlos," she said in a callous manner, "we will hear, in the morning how Audrey is doing, so drink your cocoa and try and get some sleep," she moaned.

Carlos appeared so vulnerable, like a scared little boy, so he became very obedient to mum, and drank his cocoa and went straight to bed. Mum gallivanted round Carlos, and Audrey's cottage to find some extra bedding, and eventually she found them in the cupboard next to the boiler room.

If anything mum wished she had brought her own linen from Bramwells, because, Carlos and Audrey's extra linen smelt stale. She struggled to get herself comfortable on the tiny sofa which was in the lounge. It was more like an arm chair without much room for mum to stretch her long legs, so mum kept grumbling while trying to make herself comfortable. Eventually mum, crushed out, and was getting her much needed rest, and before long Carlos was snoring away as well. In the mean time at Bramwells, Charlotte, Sophia and I were still wide awake, none of us could get any sleep, Charlotte and Sophia were scared of the old woman ghost, I was worried about mum, dad, Carlos and Audrey, so we all decided to sleep in the lounge, it was warm, cosy and it felt safe.

"I wonder what happened to Audrey?", Sophia asked in a concerned manner.

"Mum thinks, there is something weird about this cottage, face it, she is not the only one," Sophia muttered.

The fire was on, in the lounge creating a sense of cosiness, and closeness, even with Sophia who had never been that close to me and Charlotte.

"I bet mum is grumbling a lot down there at Carlos', you know how mum has always been fussy with her comforts, clean sheets and comfortable beds," Charlotte expressed with a crooked smile on her face.

"I don't want to be Carlos, right now, I bet he is getting it, poor guy, I bet she is patronising him like no other business," I guessed.

"Either that, or she is boring the hell out of him," Sophia replied.

"My guess is, she has patronised him to bed, seeing Carlos, I bet he is behaving like a little boy around her, she has always had that effect on him, he automatically becomes submissive, at the sight of her," Charlotte expressed.

Before mum left, she said dad had said that the electric had gone at Carlos', just like it did here.

"I am wondering if they are in the dark, if so, then it means there won't be much of conversation going on between mum and Carlos," Charlotte added.

Sophia and I looked at each, in a kind of mischievous way, then she shook her head.

"I bet the curses are there now, it is like invoking some spirits, they always move to where they are being talked about," Charlotte responded.

"Shall we go and sneak, just to see if mum is alright?" I added.

Sophia looked at me scornfully before saying,

"It is not a good idea, first of all, mum will go mad, and secondly, if they are sound asleep, we might stir them up, and scare them even further. When father spoke on the phone, he said, Carlos was pretty shaken up anyway, and that if we were to see him we should extra gentle with him.

All he said was, Carlos and Audrey had some information on Bramwells' past history."

"I hope, Audrey will be okay, she is the sweetest person ever."

"If it had been that vicar Simms, I wouldn't have cared less, because he is such an ass hole, he thinks he is all high and might, but all he is, is hypocrite," she swore."

# CHAPTER 4

In the mean time, dad was still wide awake at the hospital, while Audrey went through some tests. Audrey went through some cardiac tests, and they also took some bloods from her, to see whether it was something else that caused her collapse, besides her heart. Audrey started hallucinating while in hospital.

"Get those spirits away from me!" she shouted.

"They want Ed and his family, just like they devoured the Adamsons,!" she shouted some more.

Dad was trying hard to keep her calm, but with fail, soon after she started vomiting black stuff and slugs, the slugs were alive and jiggling about. "Nurse! nurse!, dad called out, he also pressed the emergency button to get attention of the ward staff.

"They are trying to kill me!" she shouted.

"Ed do you see all them shadows on the wall,? they say they are coming after me! help me Ed."

Dad was petrified, and tried so hard not to break, so he remained somewhat calm.

"I am here Audrey, and Carlos is fine, he is with Jane right now, and he looks forward to you coming home," he reassured.

Audrey looked lost in space, she was losing her mind, she grabbed dad's hand vigorously. "Remember the book, I told you about at the cottage Ed, that is the only thing that can set you and your family free from these evil spirits."

Two nurses came, both female, and middle aged, one short in stature, stout and spoke with an accent, the other was tall, chubby and was wearing thick rimmed glasses. They both appeared kind, and were very polite to dad.

"We are going to sit you upright, Audrey, we can't have you vomiting, lying flat, or else you choke on your own vomit, we can't have that now, Mrs J," the short one said in a patronising manner.

They both sat Audrey up, using one of their slide sheets, and then propped her up properly using one of the buttons on her electric bed.

"What is this you have been vomiting Mrs J? is it some of last nights dinner," she continued, utterly ignoring the live slugs in her vomit.

She continued on cleaning her up, she scooped the slugs and put them in a refuse bin, she showed no fear whatsoever. Dad got shocked by what seemed like less of care of the presence of live slugs. Dad shrugged his shoulders before questioning,

"What do you think is wrong with Audrey, and what do you make of those slugs, you saw them didn't you."

"What slugs are you talking about?" the tall nurse asked.

Her name was Jacqueline, because she wore a name tag on her uniform, and the other one was called Rita. They both seemed puzzled about what dad was talking about.

"There was no slugs," they both said simultaneously.

"Are you sure you are alright Mr Thomson?" the little nurse said.

"I am sure you have had a rough night, why don't you go home to your family, and we will look after Audrey, you know that is what we are paid to do, Mr Thomson," she continued.

Dad appeared befuddled,

'How could that be, am I losing my mind,' he thought to himself. Dad had always been a free thinker, rational, and did not believe in hocus pocus and weird satanic entities, but he was beginning to doubt his very, own essence.

"It is okay nurse, I promised Audrey, that I will stay with her throughout the night," dad replied in a hazy manner, his mind was still preoccupied by the slugs which nurses did not see.

Audrey became restless again, her eyes were bulging out, she looked frightened.

"Ed do you see those all shadows on the walls," she cried. "They are saying that, they are coming after me, and you and your family."

Dad remained calm, and replied,

"There are no shadows, Audrey, I can't see them, perhaps you should try and get some sleep."

She closed her eyes, you could tell she wasn't sleeping, because her eye lids kept flickering about. Immediately, she opened them wide again, as if a switch had been turned on, on her, she began hallucinating again.

"Ed, do you see them monks there, sat on my bed?, there is about seven of them, and Mr Adamson is there with them, as well," Audrey continued.

"There is nobody there, Audrey except me," dad said.

He held her hand till she drifted off to sleep, and before long she was in deep sleep, 'Finally,' dad whispered to himself, he gently slid his hand off Audrey and went to the nurses station to talk to the nurses.

"I have had a rough night, Audrey is asleep and I am going for a walk, and may be grab a coffee in your canteen," he told.

"That is fine Mr Thomson, I am sure she will be fine, if she wakes up we will tell her, you are around the hospital," the little nurse replied.

Dad wondered round the empty corridors of the hospital, and eventually ended up in the canteen. There was nobody there, except a few vending machines, luckily he had some loose change with him, so he purchased a coffee. He sat there alone, thinking about what was going on, none of it made any sense to him. He finished his coffee, and started drifting off to sleep, and he fell asleep, despite the discomfort of the chairs, before long he was dreaming. He dreamt, he was in the old Abbey, in its former glory. In his dream, the Abbey was painted all white, there were lit candles all over the church, and there was several monks dressed in their brown robes, and covering their heads with hoods. There was the high priest, conducting what appeared to be a ritual sermon. They were all chanting in some foreign language, which dad had never heard before, In the centre of the church, lay a young girl, of puberty age, dressed in a scarlet gown. She lay on something which resembled a sacrificial table, and at the centre of the church lay the alter, where the high priest stood, holding a big knife. The knife, was a long dagger, silver in colour, with inscriptions on it, SAC, a black rubber bend was on the knife handle, holding together feathers of a black crow. Myth has always had it that black crows symbolised death, to some myths, it is a sign of death, and re-birth, for something to be re-born, it has got die first. Seven monks surrounded the table, their faces smeared with blood, and a weird hexagram painted in black, on their foreheads. There was the sound of an old piano organ playing, in some creepy tune, the high priest moved forward towards the girl, while holding the dagger with his arms stretched up, the sharp point of the dagger facing upwards towards the ceiling. Directly above where the dagger pointed, was a painting of a young woman in scarlet about to be sacrificed by a high priest, in black clocks. In the dream, dad was an outsider, standing by the doorway of the church, he could see them, but he was invisible to them. It was like a message being given to him through a dream, on one side of the table stood an older woman, with biddy eyes, a round face and was holding in one hand, something that looked like a bible, and in the other hand she held a chalice, right beneath the girl's side of her neck, as if ready to catch any blood, to be spilt during the sacrifice. The woman was in a scarlet clock, with all sorts of weird symbols written in blood, on her face. She wore a red hood, covering her head, and then, she opened a chapter in her bible, and started reading from it in some foreign language, that dad did not understand. She walked round in a full circle; as she gave her back to dad, dad noticed that a black crow was sewn on the back part of her clock, she made another full circle, and repeated the cycle to a seventh time. The high priest gave some of silence signal, and all of a sudden the music stopped, as well as the chanting, "As above, so is below," he bellowed in a deep voice while changing position of the dagger, with the pointed part of the dagger pointed from above, turning direct to the girl.

"Out of her blood, shall new beginnings happen, out of the blood of the innocent, shall the world re-birth, and shall we regain our strength of power, money, and control of many," the high priest shouted.

The girl appeared doped out, she was drowsy and unable to fight her way out. He slit the girl's throat, and the woman, as they call her, 'high priestess', held the chalice, beneath her neck, collecting the blood from her throat into her chalice. In the dream, dad tried stopping them, "No-ooo!," he screamed but nobody heard him, he moved forward and tried to push the high priest away, but to his bemusement, they all seemed invisible, and so all his efforts seemed pointless, all he could do was watch. The girl bled to death, like a sacrificial lamb, and all they did was rejoice, and chant in a joyous manner, for their cause. They all started dancing around the corpse, in a celebrating manner, it was as if, a huge burden had been lifted off them. The organ or piano weird music started playing, as the high priestess collected blood from the girl's throat into her chalice. When the cup was full, the high priest stopped the noise again, and started giving thanks giving for the sacrifice, while they all lined up to have a drink from the chalice. Dad couldn't take it anymore, so he decided to leave the Abbey, but to his shock, the bolts were shut, and locked, so he had to watch the whole procession.

"Come over here Ed," the high priest called out to him," dad got shocked.

'So he can see me,' dad said to himself, 'how weird,' he thought.

"Now you know what we are about, join us, and we will make you worthy. We lured you here, through Audrey, and we want to thank her for that," the high priest continued.

"Don't worry about Audrey now," the high priestess said while nodding her head towards the high priest.

"She will be fine, and soon will be with Carlos, in a world that we have created for them, so join us Ed," she added.

Dad quivered with fright, "Can you see me?" he asked.

"Why should I join you? you have killed so many people, all in the name of a cult. No man is greater than the other, even in your ignorance you should know that," dad responded confidently.

The priest started moving towards dad, but dad remained put, he was fearless.

"You are not real!" he shouted, "you are not real!" "Leave him!," the priestess cried, "we have got a ceremony to perform, remember."

The high priest smirked then replied,

"Very well, so be it, we will come back to him later." She, held the chalice high up, and started praying, "Almighty gods from above, as well as below, take this offering of innocence, that we bring before you, so new life can begin."

She drank from the cup, then proceeded,

"Almighty gods, give us control, and eternal life." she continued.

She passed the chalice round, and each and every monk drank from it.

"So be it," they responded, as they drank from the chalice, last to drink was the priest.

"It is done," he said while drinking the remainder of the blood.

A new birth is happening," the priestess shouted. "Bring in our new recruits," she shouted to one of the monks, one monk stood forward, he was an albino, he took his hood down, and walked towards the priestess.

"It is done, your highness," he said.

He bowed down before her, then took the dagger from her hand, in the cult they believed albinos held a special place in their beliefs, they believed special powers lay within them, since they different from anybody else. He took the dagger and walked to some hidden chamber, where he came back with some family.

"Let me bring forward to you, the Adamsons,"

he then held the dagger upwards as he ushered the family, to the alter. The family appeared like zombies, walking in a straight line towards the alter, the dad was in the front, followed by the wife, and the six children. Mr Adamson, a scrawny, little man, with a goatee beard, moved confidently, when he got to the alter, he got the dagger off the albino monk, and said, "It is done, priest." He got to the girl lying on the table, and started carving a hexagram on her stomach, using the dagger. When he finished, he said, "Almighty gods above, we thank you for the offering, for she is one of us now."

He gave the dagger to the priest, it was facing downwards.

The priest gave Adamson a kiss on the forehead. "You are one of us Adamson," he said.

"Now you have got to sacrifice your family as well Adamson," he said, so he pointed the dagger upwards, and gave it to Adamson.

They couldn't do anything to the six children, because none of them were of puberty age, the simply stared like zombies. Susan was given a scarlet gown, like the priestess, and position was given to her, and Adamson went along with it, like a hypnotised zombie, he started dancing round the circle like the rest of them. When power was passed over to Susan from the priestess, the priestess became mother to the children, it was like role reversal. The priestess removed her scarlet gown, and gave it to the priest, it was going to be burnt alongside Susan's clothes, as she took over the role of the priestess. The priestess, took Susan's children away and led them away, to some secret chamber were they wouldn't appear again till the next sacrifice, and only then, would they be born again and join the rest of them. Susan became the new priestess, and Adamson passed the dagger on to her, immediately the priest vanished, all that was left was his black clock. Adamson reached out for the clock and wore it around his shoulders, soon after, a bolt of lightning struck Adamson, and the power was passed over to him. He raised his hands up, then said,

"Let us give thanks to our gods, for a new life has begun," he grabbed Susan's hand, and led her to the pulpit of the alter.

"It has begun! it has begun!" the monks shouted as they danced round the alter.

Dad remained silent, he tried opening the door again to escape, but the door remained bolted.

"We can all see you, Thomson, you cannot run away from this, you have been chosen to be the next sacrifice, so that you know, You cannot runaway from this Thomson, you and your family are one of us now. Audrey and Carlos cannot save you, soon they will become one of us as well," Adamson said gleefully.

Dad began to sob,

"What about the book? it can save all of us," mourned dad.

Adamson looked at his wife proudly, as if thankful for the position they have been given.

"That book is meaningless Ed," Adamson replied. "How come so?," dad asked."

"Why do you think that is, Ed!. It is because you are already dead! you are in limbo!. You and your family perished the first week you moved into that cottage, no family who move into that cottage, make it past a week. You are already dead, you and your family, perished in the fire, and guess what? you caused that fire," Adamson replied gleefully.

Dad could not look at him in the eyes, he just couldn't believe what he was hearing.

"It is a lie!" dad shouted. "You are not real, and you are already dead!" he shouted again.

"None of this is real!" he repeated.

'Soon I will wake up, and all this, would have been a horrible nightmare.'

Adamson moved towards dad with his dagger, he pointed it at dad and said,

"You are one of us now, now you have got to do what is expected of you. Sacrifice your family and we can all live eternally, including Audrey and Carlos, you will see."

"Bring him to the alter", the priestess said violently, "It is time."

The priest grabbed dad's arm and was forcefully pulling him towards the alter.

"Never! never! and never!" dad shouted.

He looked at the entrance door of the Abbey, and he saw Audrey there, calling out to him saying, "Get out of there! wake up, and don't allow them to drag you in the circle."

Just before Adamson got him to the alter, dad woke up. He was woken up by some orderly asking him, to come quick because Audrey had woken up, and was asking after him.

"Where am I?" dad shouted, "don't touch me," he shouted some more as the orderly shook him by the shoulder.

"I was there!" dad shouted in his wake.

"Tell me something nurse, am I dead?" he questioned. "Audrey is awake, and she is asking after you sir, she is a bit agitated, sorry if I startled you," the orderly said.

"It is okay really, I dozed off for a minute, and kind of lost my bearings, how is she doing? and how long has she been up?" dad asked.

"She is quite agitated, and she woke up about fifteen minutes ago, sir," the orderly replied.

Dad took a sigh, "I will come right away," he replied.

Dad got up, and headed for the ward, by then it was about 5am, the sun was rising, and dad couldn't wait for it, to be 8 am, because he had promised mum, that he would leave the hospital then, and come home. Audrey was kicking, and punching the nurses, she kept shouting screaming,

"I want to go home to Carlos!, they are going to kill him!"

She pulled her drip out, and shouted, "They are poisoning me Ed."

One nurse dashed to get a bandage, in order to stop the bleeding from her arm, where she had pulled the drip from.

"I am here Audrey," dad said, in a gentle voice, while holding her hand, in the effort to calm her down.

She sat upright,

"Get me a glass of water Ed, I feel so dehydrated," she said frantically.

Dad reached over the little table, in front of Audrey, and poured some water for her, he struggled because she was still gripping his arm.

"Here you are Audrey," he said.

She galloped the water down, then said,

"Ed, get me out of here, so I can show you the book, that can rescue your family."

Dad was too tired to bother, all he needed was to be in his comfortable bed at Bramwells.

"Mm mm," he replied reluctantly,

"I am going home, at half seven this morning, and when I get there, I am going to get Jane or one of the girls to come here and stay with you Audrey."

"That is very kind of you," Audrey replied. "Do you want to say anything to me Ed?" Audrey questioned.

"I know where you have been, because I was there, I saw you Ed, with all them monks," she gasped.

"I was in your dream," Audrey stated, "I followed you in your dream to protect you and your family. There is something I want to tell you, but now is not the time, because you won't understand. You will have to walk the path first, and then you will know what this is all about," Audrey urged.

"What are you talking about Audrey? what are you saying? you followed me in my dream?," dad questioned.

Before long Audrey became agitated again, she started pulling her hospital gown off.

"I am extremely hot!," she shouted.

"I am burning! they are burning me!"

Her skin started to blister, from the face down, and big boils appeared on her arms, and slugs were popping out from them, till they covered the whole bed. Immediately a gash of wind swept through the room, and an unseen force through Audrey in the air, tossing her up and down. Dad wasn't sure how to react, was this another spiritual illusion, or was it real. He quickly called the nurses, by then Audrey was floating on the ceiling, a couple of nurses dashed in, to their horror, they saw, Audrey on the ceiling, her eyes bloodshot.

"What in Jesus name is this? one nurse shouted, quickly go grab some security guys so we can get her down," she said to the other nurse.

"How the hell, did she get up there? she questioned. "What happened Mr Thomson? Audrey asked.

"So that is real? you mean to tell me that you see that too? that she is actually on the ceiling," dad asked the nurse, his mouth was ajar in shock.

"Get me out of hell!" Audrey shouted, "I am burning!." Two security guys came, stood on Audrey's bed and managed to bring her down from the ceiling, and made her comfortable in bed.

"Don't forget the book Ed, it is in the library," Audrey said in a drowsy manner before passing out.

"I have never seen anything like this, one of the security guys said while shaking his head.

"None of us have," one nurse replied, "quickly call do Frampton," she prompted her colleague. "Doctor Frampton is not in till 8 o'clock, but Brians is in, he is on call, I will page him," she replied.

She dashed across the room to call the doctor, the other nurse by then was checking Audrey's vital signs, she wasn't breathing and her heart had stopped again. She pressed the emergency button, for the crush team.

When they arrived, Doctor Brians was one of the team, they asked dad to leave the room while they tried resuscitating Audrey. They were in the room for a good while, before calling dad back in,

"She is alright now, Mr Thomson," doctor Brians said. "Do you mind telling me what happened, that led Audrey being on the ceiling," he questioned. "Nothing seems to be making any sense to me do, if I am going to be honest with you. It happened so fast, one minute she was agitated then the next, she was hanging on the ceiling, how she got up there do, I don't know," dad replied.

"I guess that will remain a mystery, anyway she is alright now," the Doctor responded.

They gave Audrey a sedative, that send her straight to sleep, which made it perfect time for dad to leave.

"I am going home now doc, but my wife or one of my daughters will come and stay with Audrey," he said.

"By the way Doc", dad added, while scratching his head, "I don't know whether I am imagining things, how is Audrey's skin, I saw a lot of boils covering her whole body, and live slugs coming out of them, in fact the whole bed was covered in them."

Doctor Brians looked at dad in a funny way before replying,

"Her skin is fine, Mr Thomson, I haven't heard anything from the nurses about slugs. Perhaps you should get some rest," the Doctor responded.

"Good idea, I am sure my family is waiting anxiously as well for my return," dad said. He was desperate to leave. Before long dad grabbed his coat from the chair he was sitting on, and said goodbye to Audrey who was still asleep. He got home in no time, and went straight to Carlos', mum was still sound asleep on the couch. She was disturbed by a loud knock on the door, "Who is it", she shouted. "It's me Jane," dad replied. mum jumped from the couch, and opened the door for dad.

"Carlos is still asleep, how is Audrey?" she asked. Dad sat down on one of Carlos' old settees.

"It has been a nightmare," dad replied, "I will tell you all about, after I am well rested, all I can tell you is, I have been to hell and back."

Mum got off the coutch, put her shoes on, and pushed her long black hair backwards, then tied it in a bun, she was getting ready to leave Carlos.'

"Really, is it that bad?" she wondered.

"Audrey seems to be all sorts, weird stuff as well, you might call it evil spirits, Jane, I didn't know what to make of it. She is sedated at the moment, that is the only way she can rest," dad replied.

"That is a pity, all this started because of the escapade we experienced at the cottage, perhaps you shouldn't have come here Ed, and get Audrey and Carlos involved," mum replied.

Dad stood up, and looked around while thinking,

"I know Jane, you can't cry over spilt milk, it is done now, all we have to do is deal with it. Let's go home, and we will send Suzanna over to stay with Carlos, while we get some rest, then when it's about mid-day, Suzanna will drive with Carlos to the hospital and stay with Audrey. If we take it in turns like that, it will make things easier for Carlos and Audrey," he responded. There was a moments silent, then dad said,

"Come on Jane let's go home, and we will get Sophia to get here and stay with Carlos."

Mum couldn't wait to leave, so she quickly grabbed her bag, and they left, dad locked Carlos door, and took the keys so I could get in Carlos' home.

# CHAPTER 5

When mum and dad got home, they woke me up and told me I had to go over to Carlos to stay with him for a few hours, while they took a rest from all the escapades. I didn't have time to take a bath, so I had my breakfast, grabbed my towel, a set of changing clothes, Carlos' front door keys and headed for Carlos'.

"You will be okay Suzanna," dad shouted from his bedroom, he was already in bed, and so was mum.

"Mum and I will call on you around lunch time so we can organise hospital visits, warn Carlos that he might have to go to the hospital visit as well!" dad shouted.

Before I left, I went to Charlotte's room, to tell her where I was going, and I asked her if she fancied joining me there, when she wakes up, after all Charlotte and I, we had a lot of investigations to do, so what better opportunity. "I will see you about ten, it's going to be all so exciting," Charlotte said. She was wrapped round comfortably in her bedding, it was only her little face poking out of the blankets, her eyes glistened with excitement.

"I can't wait," she called out before I closed her door shut, leaving for Carlos.'

I didn't know what kind of danger I could be walking into, mum and dad won't be there, and neither would Sophia nor Charlotte. I left Bramwell nervous, it felt like mum and dad had left me no choice but to be with Carlos. I got to Carlos' and I struggled with key trying to open the door, my hands were shaking, and all of sudden I felt extremely cold, fear was crippling me. All of sudden, my stomach turned, I felt like I was going to have diarrhoea, eventually I managed to open the door, Carlos was still in bed, thank God, because I headed straight for the toilet. I had to search around first, to find out where the toilet was, because that was my first time in Audrey and Carlos' cottage. I found the toilet, and my bowels just gave in, it was as if the fear had got the best of me that it turned my stomach contents into water. The embarrassment that I could felt, if Carlos had been awake, luckily for me he was sound asleep. I made myself a cup of coffee just to stay awake, and after, I decided to take a bath, just to freshen myself up. The bathroom lay next to Carlos and Audrey's bedroom, I ran my bath while finishing my coffee, it is surprising that the sound of running water didn't wake Carlos up. After my coffee I went to have my bath, I lay there soaking, and thinking about what was going on, then I wished Charlotte was there with me, just somebody to share the burden with. I ran a full bath, and I jumped straight into it, oh! it felt so relaxing, my mind drifted, till I fell asleep in the bath. I dreamt I was being attacked by some shadowy figures, they started pushing me under the water, to my perplexity, I woke up being forced under water by some unseen force. I struggled and struggled to keep myself afloat even though tiny as the bath felt, it felt like I was in a swimming pool, struggling to stay afloat. No matter how much I struggled, the unseen force seemed to be getting the best out of me, and just before surrendering, I heard Carlos' voice shouting, I woke up, I was petrified, I couldn't catch my breathe. I had to gain composure as I didn't want to scare Carlos to death, especially with Audrey being in hospital as well.

"Are you alright in there Jane? I thought I heard some noises."

The unseen forces disappeared, and I managed to get out of the tub unscathed. I managed to take a breathe, then I replied.

"It is only me Carlos! It is Suzanna! mum has gone home, and I have come to stay with you instead! she will be back later, I am just taking a bath, I didn't have time to take a bath at home, so I thought you will be okay with it, if I bath here instead," I shouted.

"That's fine Suzanna, I only wondered what the commotion was, that's all, Carlos shouted back from his bedroom.

"There is clean towels in the cupboard, if you need any!" he responded.

"Thanks Carlos," I responded as I was getting out of the bath.

Carlos went back to sleep, it gave him great comfort knowing that somebody was there with him, so he slept like a baby. The minute I got out of the bath tub, I noticed the bath tub started filling up with water again, even though I had pulled the bath plug when I got out of it. The whole bathroom started filling up with water, water wasn't sipping out through the bottom of the door, the door became completely sealed, and before long, I found myself swimming in the bathroom. Water filled up the bathroom in no time, it was getting close to the ceiling level, I struggled and struggled, and I was finding myself drowning, I couldn't scream for fear of disturbing Carlos.

'I could die here,' I thought to himself, 'unless if I shout for help.' Immediately I screamed,

"Help!"

Carlos woke up, and headed straight for the bathroom. He struggled trying to open the door, but with fail, that is when he went to his garage to get a craw bar, by the time he got back, the door had opened by itself, and all the water had disappeared.

"Are you alright Suzanna?" Carlos asked anxiously, "what is going on?"

"I am fine Carlos, I was having a bath, and must have dozed off and had a nightmare, that's all. I must have locked myself in, and forgot to unlock the door, sorry if I gave you a scare,"

I said trying not to scare Carlos.

"Oh! I am glad, because a lot of weird things have been happening here since last night, so I thought it might be a continuation of that," replied Carlos.

"You ought to ring your parents and tell them, you are okay, lest they will be worried sick about you," Carlos added, while appearing up send minded.

"I could lose my head easily you know, if it wasn't screwed onto my body," he added.

"Carlos, you shouldn't worry yourself so much, like you do, Audrey is going to be fine, and we are all fine. Perhaps you should ring your children, and just let them know that Audrey is in hospital. Do not scare them though, because we are here for you and Audrey," I suggested.

"Thank you Suzanna, I am not going to lose my head over it, however it is wise to call the children and inform them of Audrey being in hospital," he responded.

"Good, let me go fix something for you to eat," I said.

Carlos walked about a bit, then with slight hesitation he replied,

"I am starving, how about a cooked breakfast, there is bacon and eggs in the fridge, and the bead is in the fridge as well."

So I went to the kitchen and got busy making his breakfast, while he got himself ready. Carlos had his breakfast, and went on to ring his children, Patty, Josh, Andrea, Josh, Josephine, and Mark, who all lived miles away from us.

"None of them seem to be that concerned," Carlos expressed, after he finished making his phone calls.

"I don't know what is wrong with kids these days, they don't seem to care much about their elderly parents, the only time you see them is around Christmas and Easter and the odd wedding anniversary," he added.

Soon after Carlos finished speaking, Charlotte knocked on the door, she had come to join me, I was so excited, the thought of new discoveries, excited me. I let Charlotte in. After exchanging pleasantries with Charlotte, Carlos decided to relax in his armchair while reading the newspaper. He moved his armchair close to the window, so he could enjoy the flicker of sunshine coming through directly by the window. His lounge was small, clattered with old furniture, so Charlotte and I decided not to join him as we would have felt cramped in the little space, besides what else would been there to do for me and Charlotte, except, look at Carlos reading his boring newspaper. Carlos sat there with his newspaper and a cup of tea, he appeared way content and must have felt well pampered as well, possibly wishing Audrey should be in hospital more often so that he get a lot of attention from my family. He munched his biscuits with great satisfaction, unlike Audrey, Carlos had his teeth all intact, so chewing was effortless for him.

"Girls!" he shouted, "I know it's too early, but if you fancy, there is some wine in the cellar. I know Audrey wouldn't have agreed with me there, but here I am on my own, so for a change, I get to make decisions," Carlos shouted from the living room.

Charlotte and I looked at each other and sort of grinned, we nodded our heads to each other simultaneously with excitement.

"Thanks Carlos! that will be nice!" Charlotte responded in a loud tone so Carlos could here as he was slightly deaf, perhaps due to old age, he didn't wear a hearing aid though, Audrey did.

"There is quite a few bottles in the cellar, both red and white. Do you want me to show you where they are girls? let me finish my tea first and I will be right there," Carlos shouted. Charlotte and I looked at each again, and simultaneously shook our heads, "No, no," Charlotte whispered to me, "he will linger for ages, if you allow him," she whispered.

"No we will be fine Carlos," I replied loudly, "don't worry Carlos, you just take it easy, we are here to take care of you, and not the other way round, we'll find them," I persisted.

"That's fine girls, my home is your home," Carlos shouted in a content manner.

"Shall we go to the basement," Charlotte asked. "Good idea," I replied without hesitation.

So Charlotte and I went to the basement, it was dark, I tried switching the light on, but the light bulb was gone, so I hurried back upstairs and asked Carlos if he had any spare light bulbs.

"They are under the kitchen sink cupboard," Carlos replied.

I got to the kitchen, and got a light bulb from under sink cupboard, then hurried back to the basement. We changed the light bulb, and low and behold was dozens and dozens of wine bottles so me as aged as thirty years, they were all staked neatly in rows surrounding the four walls of the cellar.

"Let's get the oldest one," Charlotte said.

We scoured through the lot, till we found one, a red, and sixty five years old. "That's the one," Charlotte yelled.

I grabbed the bottle and took it out of its encasement, "We are going to drink to Carlos and Audrey," I said, before opening the bottle.

"To Audrey and Carlos, I wish Audrey well, through her kindness and generosity", said Charlotte.

Charlotte and I drank from the bottle, the wine tasted good, then after a few sips, it tasted funny. "What is this", Charlotte shouted, she spat the wine out.

"What are you talking about, it tastes great," I replied. Charlotte's face looked fearful, she was frowning and kept spitting. "It's blood! you try it again," she yelled.

I took the bottle from her and took a sip, it tasted different, it tasted of blood.

"Yuck! disgusting! it is blood!" I expressed, I spat it out. "What is this Suzanna? Charlotte asked, "Have we just drank someone's blood."

"So it seems," I replied, "this is revolting, I bet it's got something to do with the spookiness from Bramwell."

Before long tones of cockroaches started imaging from everywhere in the basement, they covered the floor in no time, it was spooky, between Charlotte and me, we never screamed, for fear of startling Carlos, deep down we knew and expected something bizarre to happen at Carlos'. The cockroaches were literally everywhere, on the walls, creeping out from every corner of the cellar. As if it wasn't enough, multiple rats imaged, they were black in colour, double the size of any average rat you could ever see. The rats went bizarre, devouring the roaches on the floor, Charlotte and I kept jumping about trying to avoid our feet getting gnawed by the rats. After the rats finished devouring the roaches, they started disappearing in flames, till they were all gone. "Oh! what a relief," Charlotte said, after the rats disappeared, "let's try the wine again, I bet you, the blood taste will be gone."

We tasted the wine again, and it was fine.

"Are you girls alright down there?" Carlos shouted from the lounge.

"Yes we are fine, Mr J," we both shouted, "The wine is fantastic Carlos, we opened your oldest red, I hope you don't mind," Charlotte shouted.

"I will come down there, and tell you all about the old wines," Carlos responded in a loud pitched tone.

"No we are fine Carlos, you don't have to come down here," I responded.

I looked at Charlotte, then whispered, "I think, he is coming down."

Charlotte blatantly rolled her eyes, then said,

"We don't want him here, but it seems like he is coming down anyway."

As assumed, Carlos was making his way to the basement, he got to the basement door then shouted,

"I am here girls, I will tell you a bit about my wines."

Hie Carlos, we were just about to say, that's is the best red wine we have ever tasted."

Carlos struggled a bit walking down the steep stairs from the cellar.

"All these wines, I made myself, many years ago," said he.

Charlotte stared at me then whispered,

"Oh God!, here we go again, he has written a bloody essay about it, it's going to be so boring, listening to his silly talks."

"You know girls, I started making these wines thirty something years ago, funny enough, it was Audrey's idea. We had a lot of elderflower growing in the garden, and Audrey thought of the idea of turning the elderflower into wine, and in that sense we found use for it, rather than getting rid of it, or putting it on the compost. So I went and bought a few wine kits, bought a book which teaches how to make wine, and the whole thing started from there. I have got wines made from grapes, both red and white, I have got wines made from strawberries, cherries and watermelon, as well as elderflower. Years ago I started teaching wine making to a group of elderly people, down at the hospital day centre. It was elderly people, searching to socialize with others, and some it was for respite, just an opportunity to give their carers a rest, oh! those where the days girls, and I surely miss that. Of cause now I am too old and unfit to be doing all that," Carlos expressed gleefully.

"That's some story Carlos, very interesting," Charlotte grinned.

"At the day centre, we also use to make, chutneys, jam, and pickles, Audrey used to come as well sometimes, I will have to remind her of that, when she comes out of hospital," he added.

Meanwhile at Bramwells, mum and dad were up and ready to go to the hospital for the visit, and they were going to take Carlos with them. They were outside ready to go in dad's car when vicar Simms paid them an unexpected visit. "Good afternoon Ed," he shouted as he was approaching the gate.

"Where are you off too, if you don't mind me asking, remember I promised you and your lovely wife that I will drop by for dinner."

Dad looked at mum, and with slight hesitation replied, "Oh! we are off to the hospital to visit Audrey Jones, you know our neighbours, the lovely old couple. Audrey collapsed last night, and they think she suffered a heart attack, so we are off to pick Carlos, the old man before proceeding to the hospital. Poor guy, he is so frail, and so is she, so we thought we could help a little. You know, all their children live very far away, and so we thought we should step in instead," dad said.

"I see," replied vicar Simms replied, I know the sweet old couple, they have done a lot of charity for our little community, well as your vicar, I wish her well soon."

"Thanks vicar," mum replied, "you see they are like family to us, they always used to look out for the girls when they were growing up," mum added.

"Yes, and that is very noble too," vicar Simms exclaimed. "If you don't mind me asking, have you experienced any trouble here at Bramwells of late," vicar Simms asked while shaking his head.

"This is a very small community you know, word goes round quick, you see," he continued.

Mum looked at dad in a funny way and made a weird expression as if to say don't tell him anything yet.

"What do you mean vicar?" mum asked.

"Well," the vicar began, "I heard about what happened at the hospital with Audrey, one of the nurses in our little community was working on the ward last night, and she was going round telling everybody of how Audrey went flying up the ceiling at the hospital, is that true? because she said you were there with her Ed, when it happened."

Dad became nervous, he rubbed his chin while thinking of what to say to vicar Simms, he paused for a while then said,

"Of cause I was there, I stayed with her the whole the time, I saw it, and I must say, it was something else vicar. I have never seen anything like that my whole life."

The vicar raised his eye brows.

"Well, it seems like rumours are actually real then Ed," he responded.

Mum simply nodded her head then replied,

"It is shocking isn't it vicar, however we didn't have any disturbance nor trouble here at all, isn't that right Ed."

"Yeah! that's right Jane, no trouble at all, it was Carlos who rang us when Audrey collapsed, said dad."

He appeared surprised, his eyes started wondering side to side as if in confusion, he winced then said,

"This place has got history Ed, we have got history that dates back way before you moved into this village, strong secrets that bind the village together."

Dad appeared threatened by the news, he rubbed his beard as if in disbelief.

"I understand you vicar," he smiled. He looked at mum then suggested,

"We better be off, or else we will miss the visiting time, I bet Carlos is dying to see his wife."

Mum nodded in agreement then yelled,

"We better be off vicar, we don't want to miss the visiting time, I bet Carlos is waiting anxiously for us to pick him up so he can see Audrey."

Vicar Simms stared at mum and dad as if with a warning, he paced up and down, then said,

"I would hate to see you involved in a lot of hickety pickety, an all sorts of misdemeanour's, but all I can say is I warned you. Do not involve yourselves in things that you do not understand, and things that you cannot walk out of," vicar Simms warned.

Mum and dad wondered what vicar Simms meant. Dad then replied and said,

"Well vicar, you surprise me, that this mean, one man on his self and the whole community on another, well, good day to you vicar, and give my love to your lovely wife."

Mum simply smiled and bade the vicar farewell.

"Perhaps next time or a different time, we will have a lovely dinner together vicar, sorry for the let down, but, now we have got to go to Carlos' and get him to the hospital so that he can see Audrey, he is waiting."

"Sorry vicar we would love to chat all day, but we have got to go, but drop by tomorrow evening, when we are back from the hospital visit," dad winced.

"Well, that is okay Ed, just make sure, things stay the same and that you not going round digging old bones, remember as they say, fore warned is fore armed, don't go round digging old bones, so good day to you, and surely pass my sincere greetings to Audrey and Carlos. Tell them their vicar is praying for them and that the Abbey is only a few yards away, and that is where old bones lie," he said sarcastically.

He raised his hat and made a U turn at the gate bidding mum and dad farewell. Vicar Simms started whistling as he proudly walked away, then he shouted,

"Don't forget SAC is only a few days away Ed."

Dad kind of ignored his sarcasm then said to mum," What did he mean by that Jane? you heard him right, didn't you."

"We better hurry Ed or else we will be late, and don't worry about the vicar, he is just being silly." Dad and mum got in the car, and started driving off to Carlos'. The car was difficult to drive, he was trying hard to control the steering wheel. He stopped the car and got out, that is when he realised that he a flat tyre. He hadn't even gone as far as the gate. Something had eaten through his tyre, the front tyre had a massive whole through, and the sides had been slashed by some object, possibly a knife. Somebody had spray painted on the wheel, an abbreviation which read SAC "Jane you not going to believe this! we have got a flat tyre, you better get your pretty little self out of the car because we are not going nowhere," dad said. He was so frustrated, and appeared helpless, he looked at the tyre, then shook his head after muttering something sinister. mum got out of the car then banged the car door.

"Now what! she said." "I know poor Carlos is waiting for us, God knows what Charlotte and Suzanna are facing at Carlos'," she added.

"Jane do you think we have got time to change a tyre, or shall we call a taxi?" dad asked.

"Mm, I don't know Ed, you have got a spare tyre don't you, so I suggest you change the tyre, then we will go, even if we are late, the hospital will understand and give us more visiting time," mum replied.

"Why don't you go to Carlos' and let him know, what is going on here, and that, we will be off to the hospital as soon as possible," dad responded.

He set out to changing the tyre, while mum walked over to Carlos' to inform him of the change. Dad set off, changing the tyre and mum made her way to Carlos'.

"Knock, knock, knock!" she called at the door, "it is only I, Jane."

Carlos went to the door immediately.

"I am all ready to go Jane," Carlos answered, "let me grab my little bag and I shall be out."

He grabbed his little bag full of goodies for Audrey. In the bag, was a handful of family photographs, an apple pie which Charlotte and I had baked for him, a bottle of chutney and an old cul tic magazine. On the cul tic magazine cover, read, 'how to cast spells', 'human sacrifices,' and 'as above so is below,' and re-incarnation.' It was disturbing enough, to think Audrey and Carlos read all that.

When Carlos opened the door, mum budged in. "How are my girls doing Carlos?" mum asked, "I hope you have been looking after them well, she continued. "Oh! just fine Mrs T, aren't you fine girls?" Carlos shouted, Charlotte and I were still in the basement.

"Yeah! we are alright," we replied. "We are coming up there!" she responded. We got upstairs in no time to greet mum, "Is everything alright?" I asked.

Mum looked very worried and concerned.

In the meantime, back at the hospital, Audrey was up, and back in her wits, she had no recollection whatsoever of what had happened. She was sat on her bed chatting away and laughing with mum, dad, and Carlos. The doctor had been in, gave her a clean bill of health, however he was going to keep her in the hospital for a few more days to get adequate rest.

"Your health is clear like a whistle Mrs Jones," he said. "But since you suffered a heart attack, I would like to keep you in for a few days."

Audrey smiled at the doctor, he was a young man, no more than thirty years old. He was a German, sandy blonde hair, handsome, with a fine chiselled jawline. His accent was very strong, and no doubt of a caring nature. mum stared at him then said,

"I have got three beautiful girls you know, all in their twenties, perhaps one day you will meet them when they come to visit Audrey."

Mum looked at dad and winked with her right eye, every other time she had winked, she had always winked with her lazy eye. She was born with a genetic condition which meant her right eye was always going to be weaker than her left. With careful observation, one could have easily picked up on that, her right eye was smaller, and less reactive than the other.

The doctor simply smiled then responded,

"If they are as pretty as you Mrs Thomson, no doubt I would like to meet them."

No doubt, mum had in mind, match making Charlotte with him because she was the prettiest one out of the three of us.

"When are you next on shift?" she asked enthusiastically. "The girls are free from tomorrow onwards? aren't they Ed?" mum asked dad.

"Oh yes they are," dad responded absent mindedly. "What is she doing?" dad thought to himself, "she is making a fool out of the family."

"I will be back on shift tomorrow afternoon Mrs Thomson, in the mean time if you have got any questions about Audrey don't hesitate to ask, or else leave a message for me at the reception, I will be happy to assist," he said.

Dad scratched his head for a while.

"Thanks doctor, but before you go, can I have a private word, it's about Audrey of cause," he begged.

"That's fine Mr Thomson, just follow me, there is a little quite room just round the corner," he replied.

"It was great pleasure meeting you all," he uttered before making his departure and following him behind.

He led dad to this quite room then began,

"What is it you want to talk about Mr Thomson?" he asked.

"Oh! it is about Audrey, did you or your colleagues find out what caused all that bizarreness with Audrey, for instance her flying up on the ceiling?" he asked.

The doctor seemed puzzled, he cleared his throat several times, then replied.

"I heard about it, but none of us could make any sense out of it. We don't know what caused that, clearly it isn't a medical problem, we treat Audrey for her heart condition and everything else we don't get involved in. That is what I and my colleagues concluded, why don't try talking to a priest or some spiritual person, because that is not our expertise," he exclaimed.

"I see," dad replied, I guess we should be doing just that."

"Unfortunately so, Mr Thomson, but whatever happens, do keep me informed because I would be curious to know, I do look forward to meeting your daughters though," he replied.

Before the doctor left he shook dad's hand, "Hope to hear from you soon," he uttered before leaving the room.

# CHAPTER 6

Neither mum nor dad nor Carlos remembered the young doctor's name, to them it appeared as if he was going to disappear into thin air without a trace, it bothered dad, so he decided to ask one of the nurses at the reception, his name. "Doctor Edelbert, that is his name," the nurse at the reception replied.

"I shan't forget that name," dad said before going back to Audrey's room.

"He is charming isn't he," Audrey said in a dull voice. "I bet he will be a good match to one of your daughters Ed," she whispered.

"Oh Audrey! you are here to make yourself better rather than drive yourself insane," dad responded.

"Don't be silly Ed," mum cried.

"I thought he will be a good match for Charlotte, remember you want to marry your girls to good man, well there is one, you never know!" she exclaimed.

At that time Audrey's memory started coming back, "What happened last night Ed?" she asked. "Now I remember you being here, the slugs and everything else. All this started from Bramwells, didn't it Ed?"

"Why I am here is because of that dark force which dwells in the walls of your cottage."

"Oh! the book! Carlos! did you tell them about the book?" Audrey lamented.

"Tell them about the book Carlos!" she shouted.

"Your family is in danger, and oh! has vicar Simms been to your house? He knows about the book!" she shouted some more.

Audrey held Carlos' hand then shouted,

"Please let me come home now Carlos, so that I can help them."

Poor Carlos didn't know what to do, he shook his head in dismay, took a long sigh then said, "Audrey you are meant to stay in hospital, you need your rest, let Ed deal with all that."

Mum was perplexed, she shouted,

"What are you talking about Audrey, is my family in some of danger?"

"She is sick Jane," interrupted dad.

"She doesn't know what she is talking about."

He didn't want to stress Audrey more and neither did he want to put Carlos under any pressure. "These are old people Jane," dad said.

"Let it go, whatever this is about, let us take care of it." "By the way, the lovely doctor Edelbert will be here tomorrow afternoon, perhaps the girls can visit then, hey!

Jane, what do you think," dad said trying to diffuse the situation.

He checked his watch for time then shouted,

"I guess visiting time is over hey! we better be going and tomorrow the girls visit instead, you better say your good byes to Audrey, remember we want to beat the traffic, "he expressed.

Mum and Carlos said their good byes to Audrey, leaving a very saddened Audrey.

"I can't wait for next visiting time tomorrow," Audrey whispered to herself.

# CHAPTER 7

Back at Carlos' Charlotte and I were still searching for the book and were growing tired of it. "Eww! look at all this dust, I bet this room hasn't been dusted for years," Charlotte said. Immediately she started sneezing. We searched two sides of the wall cabinets, and moved on to the last shelves, in all it had taken us two hours already, and we were beginning to lose hope of finding this book. As we got to the last shelves, Charlotte spotted a big black shiny book, titled 'the crossing between the living and the dead.'

"I think I found it Suzanna!" she shouted as she pulled it out of the shelf.

"Well, let's have a look then," I responded in an excited manner.

We sat on the floor, made ourselves comfortable because we knew we were going to be drawn to the book for ages. The first page we opened up was titled, 'human sacrifices, how to cross into the next realm.'

Just before we started reading the first chapter, we heard Carlos' voice at the front door.

"Girls it is only I, can you let me in," he said. Charlotte and I looked at each other anxiously, then I said,

"What shall we do?"

"You better put the book back quickly, and let's quickly put everything back to the way it was, or else he will know that we have been venturing in his absence."

"Why don't we steal the book, take it home, and then we can read it at our own leisure, if he finds out that it is missing, we will simply tell him that we never saw it," Charlotte replied.

"Your confidence about this, is compelling.

How do you know? For all you know, he could be one of them, and the first thing he will do after coming in, would be to search for that book," I replied.

"Let's quickly tidy up then, we can always come back again to read the book, when Carlos is out visiting Audrey. Put the book back where it was, quick!" I whispered.

Carlos knocked and knocked, we ignored him while we were putting his place back together.

"I don't think they are in." We heard Carlos shout to mum and dad, who were still waiting in their car.

"Why won't you come back with us, perhaps they are in town or something," we heard mum say. By then Charlotte and I had just finished putting everything back to where it was, then Charlotte opened the door.

"We are in Carlos! we have just come back in from the back garden, we didn't hear the car, you see," said Charlotte as Carlos walked in.

"Girls! you can come home now, if you wish!" mum shouted from the car, "I am sure Carlos could do with some rest, and time alone!" she added.

"Thank you, Ed and Jane for everything!" Carlos yelled, then waved at mum and dad before they drove off.

# CHAPTER 8

Carlos looked tired, so I made him a cup of tea and a few sandwiches, he sat on his recliner chair, his feet up, and a little table on the side of which I placed his tea and sandwiches. The recliner shared position with his' favourite settee, right by the window, so it made it possible for him to look outside with less difficulty.

"Suzanna, if you don't mind getting me a couple of aspirins from the bathroom, I have got a terrible headache," he asked politely.

"That's fine Carlos, anything else?" I asked.

Carlos was such a sweet old man that I could have done anything for him. While I was upstairs getting his pills, I grabbed a little woolly blanket from his bedroom, it was crocheted in many colours, most probably by Audrey, she was a very hands on old lady of many talents. I gave him his pills which he galloped down with his tea, then I left him all tucked up in his little blanket, oh! you should have seen him, he looked like a little baby, all cosy, sweet and innocent.

"We have got to go home soon Carlos," I whispered gently in his ear, as he gently dozed off to sleep.

"Thanks girls, I will see you soon," he muttered.

"We will lock the door behind, and post the keys through the letter box," I replied.

I closed the lounge door gently and went back to Charlotte, who was in the kitchen.

"What shall we do about the book?" she questioned, "are we taking it with us? or are we leaving it here?"

"No Charlotte, we are leaving it here, if we take it, Carlos might realise it is gone, we don't know who Carlos is, he could be one of them for all you know. We don't want him knowing what we are doing."

We left Carlos' and went straight home, Sophia was home, she had company, she had brought a boyfriend with her to introduce to the family. His name was Melvin Merry weather, he was a tall handsome young man working for some banking company, he was into accounts and finance. His family lived in our village, and funny enough his dad was the local counsellor of the town, his workplace being situated at the local town house in the town centre. The ambience seemed very appealing, they were all sat in the kitchen, mum, dad, Sophia and Melvin, drinking red wine. mum and dad had been so tired with the hospital visits, so they sought relaxation by enjoying some wine. He had dark brown hair, and a slightly thick moustache, nicely combed into perpendicular edges. He was very pale looking, possibly as a result of working in an office six days a week, and his eyes looked tired green, barely masked by his thick dark lashes. He greeted Charlotte and I with such great excitement,

"I have heard a lot about you too," he said, grinning away.

I don't know whether it was me, but I thought he seemed to have a permanent grin tattooed on his face. It was as if every time he spoke, all I could see was these perfect white teeth, big and bold. I wondered what Charlotte made of him, "I bet she don't like him," I thought.

"Why don't you join us girls, "dad said he was in such excitable mood and so was mum.

'Finally there was a suitor for Sophia,' thought mum. She ran around Melvin like he was a king in his palace. "I would like to meet those lovely parents of yours,"

mum said excitedly.

"In time Mrs Thomson," he replied proudly.

We could all tell that he was a very proud young man. After mum and dad drank their feel, they just wanted to be alone, just the two of them, so they left for the lounge, leaving us in the kitchen.

Somehow Melvin felt relieved, it wasn't about the potential in laws, there was something more, so I thought. He started questioning me and Charlotte about what we were doing at Carlos'.

"So did you find the book then?" he questioned assertively. "I beg your pardon," I questioned.

"What book are you talking about?" I questioned some more.

"Don't bluff with me, you know what book I am on about," he said in an angry tone.

"I mean the book of the living and the dead, which has laid hidden for several years. Many people here suspected that it was hidden in that old couple's cottage, but of cause there was never proof of that, but now I believe it's in there."

Immediately he grabbed Charlotte by the throat, pulled out a sharp knife from his pocket and pointed it at her throat.

"It's either you are going to tell me where it is, or else she dies, or you all die," he said.

Poor Charlotte her face turned red with fright, and so did he, that pale face turned bright red with anger.

"I warn you lot, if you scream, your whole family is dead, we don't want mummy and daddy entrenched, do we girls? The whole village will turn on you and then kill you," swore he.

Because mum and dad were absent, Melvin felt empowered in the kitchen. Sophia felt powerless, half the time she was quiet sceptical about her supernatural experiences, she didn't know whether to side with her boyfriend or the rest of us.

"Calm down Melvin, or else, I don't want to see you again," she uttered.

Melvin put the knife down, and pretended he was just merely bluffing with Charlotte.

"I nearly got you there, didn't I Charlotte, I was merely playing along with what I have heard. Do you think I will honestly believe in those bullshit stories," he smirked.

He gave a perfect genuine smile.

"Ha! ha! ha!," Sophia smirked back, "not in a million years, would I have thought of that about you," she smirked.

I could see a sense of comfort returning back to Melvin when we all laughed at his prank.

"Tell me about yourselves," he questioned me and Charlotte, "bare in mind I know a lot about you already, some from Sophia, and some from your parents. You might have been out for a few hours at Carlos', but believe me, your parents have said just about enough of what I want to know about you anyway, via the committee, of cause," he smirked some more.

Charlotte, and Sophia and me simply smiled back out of politeness of cause, we were brought up to be polite to people anyway.

"Never show vindication to people, whether they like you or not," mum and dad always used to say, and that is exactly what Charlotte and I did to Melvin Merry weather. As for Sophia, she was in love with him anyway, her sense of being was swept away from her because of the feeling of love, you might say, blinded her intuition, and there was nothing Charlotte and I could do about that.

"Shall we go and see how Carlos is?" Charlotte exclaimed.

All she wanted was to be away from Melvin so we could talk about him.

"Suzanna! are you coming? let's leave these love birds alone, and find use for ourselves elsewhere. Secretly, I am sure you would love that Melvin," she expressed.

Charlotte frowned, then grabbed my hand, leading me out of the kitchen, leaving Sophia and Melvin alone.

Whatever mum and dad sensed about him, we both sensed the same thing, we didn't want to be in his company, because none of us trusted him except Sophia, we had to break free from him in the most polite manner as possible, and we all managed to waiver away from him, without causing any hurt on his behalf.

"Excuse us Melvin!" I said, as Charlotte dragged me out of the kitchen.

"I hope we see each other soon again, I mean, many a time to come!" I shouted as Charlotte and I reached the kitchen door.

"The pleasure is all mine! it was a pleasure meeting you both!" he smirked.

"Never mind him," Charlotte cried.

"He is one of them alright! You know as well as I do, that somebody sent him to Bramwells. How come Sophia never spoke of him before, he simply, came from nowhere, and for her to announce, she is in love with him. Coincidence or what? You tell me?" Charlotte shrieked in an unapologetic manner.

"Come on Suzanna! let's get the hell out here, she said." I hesitated slightly, then followed her behind.

"Shall we go to Carlos'?, or shall we go somewhere else? I guess I didn't think of that one hey except a quick exit from Melvin," said Charlotte.

"Let's go to the front garden first, I guess you need a cigarette, then we can think of what to do hey," I replied.

"You are right Suzanna, I still got some cigarettes in my pocket anyway, we can think then."

We headed for the front garden adjacent to the living room, because mum and dad could have been in there, so we wanted to be somewhere, where they couldn't spot Charlotte smoking, because it could have been something else if they caught her smoking.

We ended up on the other end of the front garden, our living room lay at the front of the house and the kitchen at the back. We decided it was a lot easier to out smart mum and dad in the living room, than that Melvin, he was too smart, and he could have easily spotted us in the back garden, and then he could have asked, why we are not at Carlos.' It was careful calculation, we saw mum and dad smitten by the television, whatever they were watching, only God knows, they appeared well into it to bother about what was going on outside. So we managed to sneak without being seen to the other end of the front garden, if they had seen us they could have easily blown our cover, to that Melvin.

"What shall we do?" Charlotte asked as she lit her cigarette in a hesitant manner.

Melvin has been sent, for all you know, he could be here for hours, just waiting to see what we are going to do next," she cried.

After careful thinking I said, "Finish your cigarette, then we will go to Carlos', remember the book, we never got to reading it."

"That's right," she replied,

"We have got to go back to the book, if Melvin believes that we have gone to Carlos' he is not going to be inclined to stay long, he will be eager to leave early and report back to whoever had sent him."

We went to Carlos', without telling mum and dad, Carlos answered the door, let us in and then retired back into his library, he was sat there in a comfortable rocking chair looking at his books.

"I have got tonnes of books girls, feel free to look at whatever book you fancy," he said. Charlotte and I immediately reached for the shelf where the book of the living and dead lay, to our amazement the book wasn't there, neither of us wanted to ask of the whereabouts of the book. I looked carefully at Carlos who was happily rocking in his chair clutching a big black book, he had the book in the palms of his hands, flicking through it casually. Then I knew there was no way we were going to get it off him, without a reason. What we feared most was to raise suspicion off him, we didn't know whether he was one of them or not.

"What have you got there Carlos?" Charlotte asked. "It looks like an intriguing read."

Carlos simply smiled at her, then replied,

"If you think you're going to get this off me, you better think again girl, in this book lies a lot of secrets, of which, I have to learn a lot about myself. There is plenty books for you girls on those shelves," he added grinning away.

"He is not part of them," I whispered to her.

We are not going to get that book today, we have got to come again," I whispered.

"What is it about, Carlos?" Charlotte smirked.

"You know girl, I have got no idea, but I am curious," he replied as he sat there comfortably rocking away while clutching on something that we so much desired.

"Do you girls want some wine? I guess you know where to get it from," he asked.

"That's perfect opportunity to get him away from the book," Charlotte whispered.

"Oh yes, Carlos," she said.

She was hoping this was going to get him off the chair and out of the library, but he stayed put.

"Well, help yourselves girls, this home is just your home as well, you should know that," he replied.

"He is not going to move," Charlotte whispered again. "Give it up," I whispered back.

"We just have to come back again, another time because he is not going to budge an inch." "What shall we do then," she whispered.

"I guess let's go back to Bramwells, hopefully, that Melvin is gone by now."

"Good idea, let's go back, give Carlos some excuse, tell him we have got to go," I whispered.

"Well, are you going to have some wine then?" Carlos shouted.

"No Carlos, I think mum and dad are expecting us back, we didn't tell them that we were coming here, we just wanted to check on you quick, to see that you are alright. We better be heading back, we will call again tomorrow morning," she said.

# CHAPTER 9

We left Carlos' and went home, we didn't stay there that long, when we got home, to our surprise Melvin was still there in the kitchen with Sophia.

"Oh! you are back, I didn't expect you to be back so soon, in fact I was just about to leave. Did you find the book you were looking for?" he grinned.

"What book are you talking about," Charlotte questioned. We don't know of any book, do you?"

"Ha ha! the whole village know of its existence, and that it's somewhere in Audrey and Carlos' cottage. The book of secrets, that binds the whole village together, without the book the village is in conspiracy," he said.

"What are you talking about Melvin?" Sophia asked, "please don't start all that rubbish Melvin."

"Ha! ha!," he jeered again, "I am only playing with you lot, to see whether you believe all this nonsense. If you have heard about it, trust me, it is only hocus pocus. I knew that, you have heard about it already from someone, all the bizarre things, most likely from vicar Simms," he continued. "Vicar Simms never said anything that connotates anything that bizarre," Sophia replied. "Perhaps you should go now, I will not have you upset my family like that."

Sophia started pushing Melvin gently out of the kitchen and out through the front door.

"I guess I will see you again, don't hold your breathe I will call you," she said as she closed the door behind him.

Melvin shrugged his shoulders, then walked through the driveway and out of the gates feeling humiliated and, more or less ashamed.

"What on earth was he on about? do you know?" she asked me and Charlotte while shaking her head.

"What a moron, I don't think I want to see him again." "Perhaps you shouldn't see him again, he is a moron alright," I responded sharply.

"I don't like him neither," Charlotte added.

"First impressions is, I don't trust him. I believe he is a worm, trying to get into the family to dig."

"Mm, you might be right," Sophia replied.

"But I am curious to know what mum and dad think of him."

"Soon it will be supper time, we can all discuss him then, and come up with a decision or vote on what we think of him, but my bet is on, mum and dad don't like him neither," Charlotte said. "Mm, I guess we will see, I am going to my room, I have got a lot to digest," Sophia said before heading off to her room, leaving Charlotte and me in the kitchen.

"I'm tired too, I'm off to my room, it has been a long day," Charlotte said before joining Sophia upstairs.

I had no choice but to go to my room as well and rest. mum went downstairs to the kitchen soon after, and started preparing supper. This time she did not ask for any assistance from any of us, she chose to labour by herself, because it gave her personal time to think, and take in everything that was going on.

# CHAPTER 10

That evening it was roast beef and potatoes for supper, and blueberry pie for afters, it took mum a good three hours to prepare while we all relaxed in our bedrooms. She called us down for supper, that brief period of time had sped like lightning, it is funny how time seems to fly when you have got a lot on your mind. At the dinner table, we discussed Melvin, not Audrey, and not the village, he had left a whiff of unpleasant odour, in terms of personality.

"I must say, I thought he was charming to begin with, but after a few minutes, I couldn't stand the foulness and vulgar coming out of his mouth. It felt like we were his possessions, subtly introducing a form of control and superiority," mum said.

She had done it, broken the ice about Melvin, because none of us wanted to hurt Sophia any further by talking about her boyfriend.

"I think he is a messenger, send by the village people to spy on us," Charlotte said sharply and unapologetic.

Dad didn't say anything at all about him, he simply munched on his steak exquisitely and seemingly undisturbed. When it got to the blueberry pie, he became chatty, all he spoke of was Audrey.

"Audrey was in such good spirit today, don't you think Jane," he said looking at mum.

"By the way, mum took a good liking to the young doctor who saw Audrey, he is a young German, charming and with good charisma, why don't you visit her tomorrow Sophia, you might bump into him, I am sure you will have a lot in common."

This was dad's polite way of saying he didn't like Melvin. Mum responded by defending Charlotte's position by saying,

"Charlotte and Suzanna should go instead, after all you two never seem to have any plans for anything. Sophia you have got work right, and after you spend time with your friends, perhaps over the weekend, and that depends on whether she is still in hospital."

Dad smiled at Sophia then said,

"Better luck next time hey," he winked at mum, then proceeded to say, "I guess it's you two then visiting Audrey tomorrow, my suggestion is, dress well because you never know who you going to meet there, it could be Mr right," he winked again at mum.

"Ain't that right mum?" he said smiling in a crooked manner.

"I would like to visit Audrey!" Charlotte shouted, "and I am sure Suzanna would as well."

"It sounds fine by me," I responded.

"I think it will do her a lot of good having different people visit her. By the way dad, have you heard from their children, I am sure it would help her as well as comfort her that her children and grand children visit as well."

Dad scrapped his platter of pudding, sat back carelessly then responded,

"You know as well as I do that their children live far away, and they don't seem that bothered, you only see them Christmas time only, obviously they don't seem that bothered."

"According to them they are old, and just one foot in the grave, and just a pain, so it seems to me," mum expressed.

"I agree with you mum", Sophia said, "anyway Charlotte and Suzanna are going to visit Audrey tomorrow."

"Oh well dinner was very nice, but still, this is an experience to pass, I am going to bed, leave the dishes, and tomorrow is another day," mum said.

Mum left the table abruptly, "Are you coming dad," she said uncaring.

"I am coming Jane," dad replied, "I know what you are saying, we all need personal time to reflect, by the way, dinner was fantastic, more infatuating than this shit we are dealing with," he said.

Mum left for bed, then followed by dad. We became inclined to leave the dinner table, leaving dirty dishes on the table, and followed suit upstairs, to bed. Charlotte was the last to leave the dining room, she took a good look round before turning the lights off and going to bed, like the rest of us. We all went to bed I could swear, none of took to sleeping well, we all laid there wide eyed, contemplating and anticipating something to happen. It was mum and dad who settled into sleep first, before long they were sno ring away, Sophia laid there in her bed, wide eyed, as if waiting for something, so did Charlotte and I.

# CHAPTER 11

It got to about midnight, then the three of us awoke, heard footsteps coming up the stairs. It couldn't have been an intruder because dad had checked and double checked the front and back door, whether they were locked or not, before going to bed. The noise came from downstairs, we heard footsteps come upstairs, the footsteps sound became more and more subtle as they came upstairs. Dad woke up, got out his bedroom holding a fire porker which had always stood right next to the fireplace in his bedroom.

"Are you alright girls!" he shouted.

He went in Charlotte's room first as it was right next to his bedroom, Charlotte was up, her little face poking out of the bedding in a frightful manner.

"I seem to be," she replied. "I heard that noise too dad, what was it?" she asked.

"I don't know dad replied.

He looked round her room, searched the wardrobes, but there was nobody there.

"Stay alert, I will check in Sophia's room and Suzanna's, then the bathroom," he said.

He went into Sophia's room, but found nothing, then the bathroom and lastly my room, and still found nothing.

"I remember locking all the doors last night before going to sleep," he said to me.

"I don't know dad, if you are going downstairs, I better come with you," I said.

"Your mum is fast asleep, I bet she can sleep through anything. If you are coming downstairs with me, make sure you stay behind me, alright," he whispered.

I put my dressing gown on, slippers, then followed dad downstairs. He went to the kitchen, and grabbed a big, sharp knife from the drawers.

"Here you are Suzanna, take that, just in case," he whispered.

I took the knife from him, I was scared, in the event of something happening, I didn't want to use it. He then walked into the music room.

"Be careful dad," I whispered while following him behind.

All of a sudden we found ourselves tip toeing inside our own house like strangers, it was petrifying. There was nobody there, lastly it was the living room, the door was shut, he opened the door gently, and me behind him as planned. I held the knife pointed as if ready for attack.

"Be quite," he whispered.

He walked in the living room and so did I, to our surprise we saw Melvin bended over going through our stuff, mainly paper work and books. Papers and books were scattered on the floor, nearly covering the whole floor.

"What are you doing in my house!" dad shouted, he pointed the porker at him, then grabbed him by the throat. "What the hell do you think you are doing in my house, you little shit, get the hell out of my house," he screamed.

"But before you go, you owe me an explanation, frightening my family like that," he shouted some more.

You and I need to talk."

Melvin appeared unshaken, he looked as if he was in some form of a trance, more like a zombie.

"Please don't hurt me Mr Thomson, I can explain everything," he cried.

"You better do, or else you are going to jail. Do you know what breaking and entering is? son. You going to explain yourself to the police! and wait till your proud parents hear of this! you are going to be sorry son!" dad shouted.

"It's more complicated than you think, Mr Thomson. Soon enough you will understand, I was merely sent here, who sent me, I will never tell, you can send me to jail if you like," he replied.

He didn't seem to show any fear nor remorse for breaking into house.

"Out of curiosity, how the hell did get into my house," dad asked.

"You might think, you locked up every door in your house last night, but your hallway window was open, that is how I got in, Mr Thomson. I knew that you never open that window, but when I came here yesterday, I made sure that I opened it so that I could come back later when you are sleeping. Sophia told me about the window yesterday, I knew you will never check there, with the window disguised nicely behind heavy curtains."

"Okay! now we getting somewhere, pick all those papers up and put the books back where you found them, then we can talk," dad responded, his anger wearing out.

"You could have been dead, I could have killed you with this porker, or my brave daughter there," he pointed at me, "could have killed you with that knife in her hand."

Melvin picked up all the papers he had scattered all over the floor, and put the books back onto the shelves.

"What are you looking for?" dad asked.

"Suzanna! go back to bed! This young man and I need to talk, put that knife back in the kitchen," he yelled.

I looked at dad, he was full of stress, his colour was gone, I debated whether to leave him alone with this menace of a man.

"I will be fine Suzanna, go to bed," he fashioned.

I looked at dad, then Melvin, shook my head, then went upstairs, I took the knife with me though to bed.

I didn't sleep, I was wide awake, eves dropping, but I didn't hear much. I could hear muttering, nothing was coherent since I was upstairs and they were downstairs, and still worrying about dad's safety, my knife was ready, if he were to threaten father.

I could have easily sneaked into Charlotte's room, my partner in crime, but I didn't want to scare her more than she was already, so I stayed put in my room, waiting.

"Mr Thomson, there is a myth in the village, of the village curse, I don't know whether you have heard of it," Melvin began.

"The story goes, there is a book somewhere, either here in your house or at Carlos', the book is about the living and the dead, the cross over. That is the reason why I am here, I was just curious to see whether the legend is real, and so Sophia came along in my life, I couldn't resist to find out about this book, that is why I am here," he explained.

"Okay," dad said, "but you haven't explained, who sent you here? that is all I want to know," he shouted.

Dad got up from the seat which he had made himself comfortable, and grabbed Melvin by the collar, "Who sent you here?" he shouted loudly that I heard him from upstairs. "I can never tell you who, Mr Thomson, in as much as I would like to. My life could be in danger, I would rather go to jail," Melvin replied.

"Fine," dad replied, "you are going to jail then son."

He picked the phone up and called the police, Melvin didn't even look scared, he didn't try to run away neither, partly because I had seen him as well so dad would never be short of a witness. In no time the police came, hand cuffed Melvin and led him away. All this happened while we where upstairs, and mum sound asleep.

"Phew! dad cried, as Melvin was led away in a police van. "Thank you officers!" he shouted as they led Melvin away, "we can sleep well at last," he yelled, then shut the front door with a loud bang.

If dad only knew what was going to happen, it was nothing like good night's sleep. After Melvin was taken by the police, dad went back to bed and urged the rest of us to go back to sleep. "Now the intruder is gone, you have earned yourselves a good night's sleep," he said as he matched back to his bedroom.

We all followed suit, and before long we were out for the couch, not bothered about anything and not even Melvin. 'Sleep heh!' I thought to myself, 'it is not to be found in this cottage, not tonight anyway.'

I felt as if something big was about to happen, I felt like a big storm was about to break. I chose not to share my thoughts with anyone, except wait for whatever that was coming next. Then, thereabout four thirty in the morning, commotion started again, we heard a loud noise coming from upstairs, it was coming from Sophia's room. It sounded like a loud groan from a grown man,

"You are coming with me!" the voice sounded, it was so loud that it woke the whole family up including mum who normally sleeps through anything.

Dad jumped out of his bed, by then mum was awake as well, "Ed what's all this?" she cried half asleep.

"I don't know sweetie, why don't you go back to sleep, just leave everything with me, I am sure it's nothing," dad replied.

He didn't want to fill her in with what had just happened, if mum had known of Melvin breaking in and eventually led away by police, none of us could have found any peace from her, nor enjoy the luxury of a few hours sleep. So mum went back to sleep just like that, she was easily fooled, or she was too lazy to be bothered with what was going on. Sophia started screaming, the ghost of the old woman had appeared again in her room, except this time she was accompanied by some children. All of a sudden we could hear birds flapping outside in the garden, it sounded like there were tonnes of them. I went and got Charlotte out of bed, she was awake anyway, like me, she hadn't been able to go back to sleep, after the fiasco with Melvin. We looked out of her bedroom window, and we saw tonnes of black crows perched everywhere in the back garden, some were flapping right by her window, it seemed like there were everywhere surrounding the cottage.

"Dad! dad! Charlotte screamed, come and see this."

In no time dad was in Charlotte's room, and we were looking in wonder at these birds,

"What is all this!" he screamed, "I bet it's got something to do with that Melvin! I knew it! I knew there was something off with that Melvin, right from the minute I set my eyes on him."

"What shall we do dad?" I asked, "it's not like, you are going to call the police on this one."

Dad looked very puzzled, for the first time in my life, I saw him appear very helpless, he looked very vulnerable. He started pacing up and down, trying to think of what to do. "Whatever you do, try not to wake your mother up,"

he whispered.

"You know what she is like, she will make everything ten times worse, so trust me, let's deal with this our own. If she catches on, she catches on, we will have no choice but to fill her in with what is happening, but in the mean time, it is all hush! hush!," he whispered cautiously.

Sophia screamed again, this time a lot louder, we hurried to her room, to our astonishment, she was being sucked under the bed by some unseen force. We saw the old woman, holding hands with six children, the children were pointing at the fire place in her room, and in an echoey manner saying, 'help us, we are trapped.'

Dad reached out to Charlotte, by then half her body, had been dragged under the bed, he grabbed her arms, trying to pull her upper body in vicinity. He struggled and struggled, then yelled,

"Help me pull! we are losing her."

Charlotte grabbed dad's waist, and I held Charlotte's waist and started pulling as well, we didn't want to lose Sophia at all. We pulled and pulled, screamed and yelled, and at the same time being cautious not to wake mum up, till we got to a point past respecting mum, and started yelling out loud. To our astonishment, even that did not arouse her, so individually we discarded the courtesy, 'if she wakes up, she does, but our sister meant everything to us, and dad was not willing to lose a daughter out of courtesy. "Forget about mum!" Charlotte yelled, "I would rather she catches up with what's going on and be destructive, than us losing our sister," she swore.

We fought, and fought, pulling Sophia, but unfortunately it proved to be a fight we lost, she disappeared beneath the bed right before our eyes. Dad desperately reached out for her to no avail, Sophia simply vanished under the flooring.

"She has got to have gone somewhere," he cried.

"Let's us move the bed, and the carpeting, she is somewhere there!" he yelled.

As he moved the bed the other way. Charlotte and I had no choice but to help him. I helped him push the bed to one side, then started unrolling the carpet from one end, we wanted to see if there was a secret passage beneath the carpet, and of cause there was. When we unrolled the carpet we saw a drainage chamber just like Charlotte and I had seen at Carlos' house.

"She is somewhere in there," I told dad.

"Charlotte and I saw one of these at Carlos' house, and it led us to the Abbey ruins, quick dad!" I yelled.

Dad immediately rolled the drainage chamber over, none of the family had seen one of these besides Charlotte and I, what reason could we have? except at Carlos', when everything lay beneath the carpets of Bramwells. Dad,

Charlotte, and I, saw the old woman and some children, before we could ask them, what they wanted, they vanished into thin air. Sophia's room was covered in smoke, we could even smell the charcoal smell in her room.

"What do you want from us?" dad shouted.

"Was that real! please tell me, I am dreaming, this is just a nightmare!" "What about the crows?" he asked.

"You and Charlotte should go outside and see what the crows are about, while I go down that drain and see if I can find Sophia, if I don't return in a few minutes, go to the Abbey or Carlos', because since, as far as you are concerned these drains either lead here, Carlos' or the Abbey. If I don't return," dad gasped, call the police."

He lifted the lid of the drain, and started his way down. "But if you don't return, Charlotte and I will make our way down the tunnel," I expressed. "Get a torch dad!" Charlotte yelled.

She yelled because it was time for no pretence in regards to mum's peace of mind, it was a time of choice, Sophia's life or mum's hysteria.

"Yeah! you are right," dad responded.

Charlotte got the torch for dad, and he proceeded down the tunnel beneath Sophia's room. How could we have known it existed when the whole cottage was covered in carpets, the bathroom was different because it was laid in parka flooring, and where the drainage chamber was situated, there was a subtle lifting handle, it could have been anything, decorative even, and no one could have told any difference.

"Let's go outside now and see what is happening out there," Charlotte said.

When we stepped out of the cottage, tonnes of crows came flapping in our faces, it was very difficult fending them off, we could barely see. All I could see was the garden completely devoured by these birds, All the plants had been eaten away, the front lawn patchy, and the drive covered in bird poo. "Sophia must be at the Abbey, remember what happened to me at Carlos', if she is not there she will be at Carlos'," Charlotte added.

"Then let's go to the Abbey, we might find them there," I suggested.

"Poor Sophia," I said, "I wonder what is happening to her right now, quick! let's go," I prompted Charlotte.

The Abbey ruins were a good five minute walk away from home, when we got there, the place was as silent as the grave, it was a big place covering a few hundred yards square footage. It was pitch black, Charlotte and I did not have a torch because dad had taken the only torch in the house with him. We wondered round the Abbey going through one dilapidated passageway into the next, but there was no sign to be seen of Sophia or dad. I saw a ghostly figure of a man dressed as an old monk, he was wearing a brown gown with a hood covering his head. I could see because it was a clear night, with a full moon, perhaps the full moon symbolised whatever was happening to our family, especially knowing that cult rituals and full moon tend to synchronise.

I called out to Charlotte, "Over here!" She came immediately.

"Have you found them!" she yelled.

"No," I replied, "do you see that man over there, in brown?"

She looked, then puzzled, she replied, "Yes I do, who is he?"

"Let's follow him," I suggested.

We followed him, as soon as we got close to him, he moved away. We followed him to the other end of the Abbey, and there, we saw dad, he was surrounded by these ghostly figures of monks in brown gowns, and amidst them was a man in a red gown. The man in red appeared to be conducting a form of ceremony, and dad appeared to be in a form of trance, he looked as if he was very comfortable being around these figures.

"Let's wait and watch from a distance," I said.

"We don't know who these people are, and we don't know whether they are dangerous or not," I said.

So Charlotte and I hid behind some old pillar, and watched. The man in red was holding a red gown, and was ready to pass it on to dad, that is when I felt we should do something and make our presence known, and disrupt whatever ritual they were conducting. Dad stretched his arms out to receive the garment, that is when Charlotte screamed.

"Dad! dad! don't! We are over here!"

He heard her, and then appeared shocked from what was going on, he came out of the trance, and ran from them people.

"Don't go after him yet! he will return by himself!" the man in the red shouted.

"Let him go, soon enough he will realise that there is no running from this."

Dad joined us, "Where is Sophia?" he asked, "I couldn't find her."

"Who are those people dad?" Charlotte asked. Dad was still appearing slightly confused.

"I don't know them girls, I wish I did, but I don't. I don't know what was happening to me, it feels like I have just woken up from a nightmare, said dad."

"We still can't find Sophia," said Charlotte.

We searched throughout the Abbey ruins, and still we couldn't find Sophia.

"I don't get this, where could she be," dad said, "I followed the tunnel route and it led me here, and yet she is not here." "Those creatures better not have captured my daughter, I don't what they are, human or not human."

"I think I know where she might be. At Carlos'. Trust me dad," I said.

"That's right dad, we have been through these tunnels before," Charlotte confirmed.

"Quick! we better hurry," dad responded.

Tears started streaming down his cheeks, he bent over helplessly and started sobbing.

"Is it my fault? it is all my fault!" he cried.

"Where have I ever wronged you girls? I don't get it! it is all my fault."

He curled into a ball on the dusty floors of the ruin, he was motionless, and sobbed and sobbed.

"Come on dad! let's go!" I shouted.

"it is not your fault, it is nobody's fault, but we have got to find Sophia, we don't want anything happening to her, the sooner we find her the better."

"Just think of your family dad, you have got to get up now, and let's go," Charlotte yelled.

Dad remained there motionless, lamenting.

"Let's grab him, and get out of here," I said to Charlotte.

I started seeing Charlotte breaking, so I had to snap her out of the feeling.

"Come on Charlotte! I need you to be strong, dad is breaking, and not you as well," I shouted.

She regained her momentum, and we grabbed dad from the floor and led him away, supporting him, shoulder to shoulder. The minute we left the Abbey ruins, a gush of air swept through, and we saw tonnes of birds flapping in the sky and flying towards the Abbey. We watched them fly over to the Abbey and then disappear into thin air. We got home, searched for Sophia there, but she wasn't there, that is when we headed for Carlos'.

"I hope you girls, know what you are doing," dad said. He followed us behind, I think he was beginning to trust us, he handed the torch to Charlotte who led the way. We got to Carlos' cottage, knocked on the door, poor Carlos' must have been fast asleep. Dad banged on the door, till he opened the door, the whole cottage was dark, we had forgotten that Carlos' electricity wasn't fixed yet, he had candles in every room and matches was always at hand. "We are looking for Sophia, and we believe she is here, said dad.

"Why don't you come in," Carlos said, he was holding a torch.

"I haven't seen her," Carlos said.

He was rubbing his eyes, wearing old tatty drawers, and vest.

"We need to search your bathroom Carlos, don't be alarmed, I will explain everything later in the morning," dad said in a husky voice.

"Okay, that is fine Ed, you know where the bathroom is," Carlos replied subserviently.

"I appreciate Carlos, if it was your daughter missing I am sure you would do the same," dad said.

He went upstairs to Carlos' bathroom with me and Charlotte following behind, an so was Carlos, who appeared perplexed.

"What made you think she could be here Ed?" he asked. "I will explain everything later Carlos, right now you wouldn't understand anything, and neither have I got the time to explain," dad replied.

We got to the bathroom, and there in the corner of the bathroom was Sophia, sobbing her eyes out, she was terrified.

"Dad! dad!" she cried, "I thought I wasn't going to see you ever again. I have been to hell and now back, I am so terrified," she sobbed as she reached out to hug dad.

"I was pulled down the bed dad, how it happened, I have got no idea, it felt like I was dreaming, and yet awake, if you know what I mean," Sophia expressed.

"It's good to see all of you," she cried.

Dad hugged Sophia back, his eyes streaming with tears of joy.

"Oh! girl, I thought I had lost you, it is all my fault," he cried as he rubbed his hands gently on her hair.

Thank your sisters, somehow they knew where you were."

Charlotte and I reached out or Sophia and gave her a hug.

"Thanks Carlos," dad said,

"Remind me to fix that electrics of yours, it is funny that we completely forgot about it, with all the happenings, but for now we thank God that we are all alive hey," he said as he led Sophia down the stairs.

Charlotte and I simply followed behind, we were just happy to have our sister back, we got to the front door, right behind dad and Sophia.

"You know Ed, I don't know what this has been all about, but I feel you know best, and that it was all meant for the good," Carlos muttered while nodding his head in agreement with whatever was going on which in no doubt knew nothing about.

He was always loyal to mum and dad.

"I shan't bother you anymore Carlos," dad said.

"You better get yourself back to sleep and we will talk in the morning, and lock up behind yourself."

"I will do Ed, you know best," he responded.

From the moment we moved into Bramwells, Carlos had always looked up to mum and dad, he had always treated them like they were his own children, and like wise, mum and dad treated Carlos and Audrey like their parents. We left Carlos' and went home, none of us had much to say to one another, it was all left to Sophia to say where she had been. We sat in the kitchen, contemplating, then Sophia begun,

"When I got sucked under the bed, I was led to these dark tunnels where I felt no control of whatsoever of what was going on, I found myself alone at these crossroads, and immediately the wind blew me in one direction, and I found myself at the Abbey ruins. I wasn't there for long, but while there, there was dozens of old monks, all dressed in brown, surrounding me and chanting in some weird language. 'She is not ready yet,' they whispered to one another, 'send her back', "that is how I found myself in Carlos' bathroom."

"I was scared, and I did not know what to do, obviously, I did not want to alarm Carlos, with everything Audrey is going through at the moment. I was contemplating on what to do, and at the same time, paralysed, that is when you came in. I thought I could die, and I thought this force could suck me in to a different unknown that

I could never return from, so thanks to you guys, you came to the rescue," she said.

Charlotte, dad and I looked at each other, without much are do, Charlotte replied,

"Aren't we all tired, we could all do with some rest, and we will talk in the morning."

"I agree," dad said, "I have had a crazy last two days, and I believe it's the same for Charlotte and Suzanna, so I am off to bed."

Dad went to bed, then followed by Charlotte, Sophia and I.

# CHAPTER 12

Next morning was bright and fresh, mum and dad where up first, followed by Charlotte and I, Sophia remained in bed, and so dad had to call up the local municipality, asking for an off sick day on her behalf.

"How was your night?" mum asked.

"I slept like a log," she said yawning away.

She was in oblivion of the happenings of the night before, none of us wanted to fill her in, for fear of that turbulence and confrontation should bring, she wasn't cut out for things like that. "We all slept well," Charlotte and I replied simultaneously, dad simply glanced at us at nodded in agreement."

"Sophia has taken a day off work," said dad.

"She is too tired, with all the happenings with Carlos and all, I thought it will do her some good to take a day off work," dad said.

"You know, I had a horrible dream," mum said.

"I dreamt Melvin had broken into the cottage, searching for something, and you managed to get him arrested, Sophia was defending him, saying it wasn't his fault because some people had sent him, that is when I woke up."

"It is just a dream, don't worry about it," replied dad.

"If you say so Ed," she responded.

"Who is for pancakes!" she asked, her voice was sounding nervous, she fiddled with the saucepans, her hands were trembling from nerves.

"We all want pancakes!" I replied, "and we are all alright," I instigated.

"Don't you want pancakes!" I asked dad, and Charlotte, of which they both agreed.

She went on to make pancakes, of which none of us ate, we were thinking of the experiences we encountered. Dad gave an excuse before disappearing off to work, and Charlotte and I simply said we were not hungry, mum couldn't understand.

"Never mind hey!" she said,

"It's not the first time you have gone without breakfast." She cleared the table without complain, then said, "I wonder how Carlos is holding up? perhaps you two should check on him, before we take you to visit Audrey, in the afternoon. "Are you okay mum, you seem kind of jumpy this morning," Charlotte asked.

Mum was drying the dishes, she dropped a plate which shattered on the floor, her hands were still shaking uncontrollably.

"I am fine, just a bit spooked by the dream I had. When are you seeing Melvin again?" she asked Sophia.

Sophia looked at me and Charlotte, then replied,

"I don't know mum, it is early days, I guess I will see hey, but you need some rest mum and stop worrying yourself sick."

"Why don't you put your feet up, and we will finish clearing up," Charlotte said.

"Thanks girls, I will do just that, you know with all this Audrey, Carlos thing, it gets me worried," she replied then sat down on one of the kitchen chairs.

With Melvin in prison, I secretly suggested to Charlotte and Sophia that we pay him a visit, he seemed to know something about what was happening to us.

"I don't think it a good idea," Sophia whispered.

"I am incredibly scared, none of us know who sent him here in the first place, they could be highly dangerous people, perhaps even a cult."

"What about the book Charlotte?" I whispered. "We could go to Carlos' and get the book." "Oh yeah," she replied.

"We could go there soon after finishing clearing up." "What book are you talking about?" Sophia enquired. "We will tell you about it when mum leaves the kitchen,"

Charlotte replied.

Mum was looking well rested, drinking her coffee. "What are you girls whispering about?" she said.

"I better be out of your way and perhaps do a bit of gardening, it will get my mind off thinking about Audrey and Carlos."

"It sounds like a great idea, call us if you need any help," I remarked.

"Will do," she replied then left the kitchen without finishing her coffee.

"The book we saw at Carlos' is a book about the cross between the living and the dead," I told Sophia.

"Melvin spoke of the book, that is what he was looking for when he broke into the cottage. Vicar Simms spoke of it as well, he was warning us, not to temper with it, but we have got to get that book, if we are going to make sense of what is happening here and at Audrey's as well."

"If this is true, then it means, our lives could be in danger," Sophia sighed.

"I want to see this book. I can come with you to Carlos', but I can't visit Audrey, not today anyway, I am too tired to bother with her as well."

"Very well," I replied.

We finished clearing up and headed for Carlos' who was still in bed. We knocked and knocked at his door.

"Wake him up! if we have to," Sophia expressed.

We knocked and knocked some more till Carlos' came down and opened the door in his old drawers and tatty vest. "Good morning girls, is everything okay?" he said with a warm smile on his face. "Come on in."

He was very welcoming as usual, and didn't complain a bit. "Do you want some tea?" he said.

"But I have got to get dressed first, so bare with me." He went upstairs to get dressed, while Charlotte, Sophia, and I made ourselves comfortable in his lounge waiting.

He came back down wearing some old clothes, he had always looked tatty anyway, so it was no surprise. To be polite, we accepted his offer of tea, while he made the tea, boiling the kettle on some old burning stove, we were whispering to one another on how we were going to get the book from his library. We were waiting with anticipation, Carlos came in holding a tray, his long grey beard barely touching the cups of tea, and on the tray was a plate full of biscuits, he loved his biscuits. He sat comfortably on his armchair by the window, then said,

"What can I do for you?"

Charlotte, Sophia and I looked at each other, then Charlotte winked at me.

"We were worried about you, and we are here to ring up the electric man, since you have been out of electrics for a while now. Dad had forgotten about it, you know everything happening so fast, so he reminded us to ring up the electric man for you," Charlotte said.

"Oh yes, that is very kind of you, Audrey is getting better, and I think they are going to discharge very soon from the hospital. I wouldn't want her to come home to no electrics."

We sipped on our tea, buying time to win Carlos over, so that when we ask after the book, he would be in a relaxed state. We talked about mundane stuff, his garden, his children and grandchildren, all in the effort of putting his mind in a relaxed state; so that when we ask for the book, he would simply be compliant. He became quiet relaxed.

"You know something perplexes me," he paused,

"All this happenings, there must be something more to it," Carlos expressed.

He paused again, then proceeded,

"Perhaps I am just an old man imagining things. When I married Audrey, I married into her family, because I had no family of my own, you see, I was adopted, and grew up in different foster homes till I found my way into the big wide world out there. I got a job as a blacksmith, till I met Audrey, her family owned this place, we simply inherited it from them when we got married. For a while Audrey and I lived with her parents, till they passed away, and that is when we decided to start a family of own."

Carlos got up and reached out to some old cupboard, he grabbed an old photo album.

"I will show you pictures of what it was like then," he paused again,

"Do you mind topping up my tea Sophia," he gasped. "You know Sophia is a special name around here, I mean, in the village."

Charlotte and I looked at each other, then raised our eyebrows simultaneously, as if it were a sign, that finally we were getting somewhere with our mystery searches.

He showed us the photo album, but nothing seemed to appear out of the ordinary, except the fact that it was along time ago.

"Perhaps we should come back to the album another time," Charlotte whispered in my ear, "more so when Carlos is out," she added.

"I agree, I am sure, if we take our time studying the album, we are bound to see something," I whispered back.

"Oh! those were the days," Carlos said proudly. "However, back then people used to talk about your cottage. There was a tragedy that befell this family who lived at your cottage, this was over a century ago. The dad was the priest of the Abbey, as you know now it's all ruins, they say he burnt his whole family in the cottage including himself. They say he was delving with some cult, and that the cult made him do such atrocity to his family. Rumours have it that, he lives on, at the Abbey, and that any other family that were to move into the cottage will die in a same way."

Carlos paused again then begun,

"Call it crazy or what, I might just be an old man talking nonsense, but the legend seems true. Audrey and I did not want to scare you, we wanted you to be happy in your new home, that is why we did not say anything; we chose not to believe the myth at all."

Charlotte, Sophia and I looked at each other in dismay, but somehow we believed him.

"It is funny though, that every family that has lived in your home before you, I mean in my time here, they all perished in some fire accident. I am surprised you were not told that, when you bought Bramwells. The cottage went on fire, and they rebuild it again, and again, till you moved in there," Carlos said.

"Mmm, that is something," Sophia said, "please tell us more Carlos," she prescribed.

Carlos sipped his tea gently then continued,

"Since I moved here with Audrey, so far there has been seven episodes of fire accidents in your cottage. Some families who moved in there, did not last as long as three days, they complained of weird phenomena's and quickly moved out, even leaving all their possessions in there. Of cause Audrey and I never really believed in all that stuff, as far as we were concerned the fires were all accidental."

"Anyway, enough of that silly talk," Carlos gasped. "You said you are here to ring the electric men, why don't we do that hey."

He got up, went to a chest of drawers then started fiddling with some paper work.

"I have got an electric bill here! now you can make that call," he said.

"I don't know why I didn't ring them up myself. I guess it is because Audrey used to take care of all the household stuff."

Sophia got the letter from him, went out to the hallway where the phone was on the wall, and she rang the electric company. It was going to be a couple of hours before they arrive to fix the power, so we had to hang around till then, and there was still the book to find.

"They will be here soon Carlos," Sophia said.

"I remember Audrey mentioning something of a book that has got history of the village and it's mythology, she said the book was here. Do you know anything of that Carlos?" Charlotte asked.

She was trying to trick Carlos to showing us the book. "I think it might be useful to us, so we can understand what this place is all about."

"I have heard of the book," he replied.

"But I have got no idea of it's where about, I don't think it is here. Last I heard through rumours of cause, was that it was being held at vicar Simms' home, and that he won't let anybody near it."

I looked at Charlotte, then Sophia, we all winked at each other, that is when Charlotte whispered in my ear.

"He is lying, he must know a lot more than he is making out."

"Why don't we try looking in the library, it might be in there, you have got so many books in there, you never know what we might find," I suggested.

"Oh! there is nothing in there, I tried looking myself but I couldn't find any book of secrets about this village. But you girls are welcome to look at any books that Audrey and I have in that library," he said.

Carlos appeared so calm and collected when he told us that lie, but however we chose to go to the library anyway.

We searched through the books, which were carelessly placed on the book shelves, but had no luck finding this big black book.

"He must have moved it, I think he is lying, he knows a lot more than he is making out, or possibly hid it, Charlotte expressed.

"Perhaps we have to wait till he visits Audrey in hospital, we will house sit for him, then we can rampage through the whole house for that book."

"He couldn't have hidden it elsewhere except within this house," Sophia said.

"Later on today Charlotte and I are going to visit Audrey at the hospital, so it has got to be tomorrow when Carlos is out," I said.

"Well, did you find anything useful girls?" Carlos shouted from the living room.

"Not really," I shouted to Carlos.

Then there was a loud knock on the door, of cause it was the electric man, so I let him in. He was tall, lanky, and grey faced man of middle age; he came in with a box of tools and was wearing a head torch on his forehead.

"Carlos! it is the electric man!" I shouted.

Carlos got up, greeted the man and lead him to the basement where the mains electric box was, this was an opportunity for Sophia to quickly search his settee for the black book; and unfortunately it wasn't there.

"Where could he have hid it?" she asked.

"It might be in his bedroom, do you think I will have enough time to go search in there before he surfaces from the basement?" she asked.

"You can try," Charlotte grinned, "we will stall him if he happens to surface before your return."

Sophia then dashed upstairs to his bedroom, there was so much stuff lying around on the floor, books, clothes, toiletries, anything and everything; it was like walking into a rubbish tip. Sophia did not know where to begin searching, so she started with the wardrobes, then the drawers, and lastly the floor. She ravaged through the rubble so fast, that she wasn't even looking carefully, for all you know, she could have easily passed the book. In the mean time down in the basement, which was dark and dingy not having a window, the only bit of lighting was permuting from the torch, Carlos showed the electrician the electric mains box. It was covered in cobwebs, and dust, a sign that it had not been touched for years. He opened the box, after clearing off a few cobwebs, he saw where the problem was coming from.

"When was the last time this box got opened? It seems like centuries, perhaps we shouldn't meddle with ghosts from the past," he jeered.

"Ha! ha! very funny, "Carlos responded.

He got his screwdriver from his tool box, to unscrew the box, a bolt of lightning came from nowhere and struck him down, he fell to the ground unconscious, and the electric box caught fire.

Carlos was in shock, "Help! help!" he shouted.

He removed the torch from the electricians forehead and tumbled upstairs, he was out of breath when he got to the library, where Charlotte and I where.

"Help! help!" he yelled again, by then he was grabbing Charlotte's hand.

"Quick! I think he is dead! he gasped.

Charlotte and I were perplexed.

"What's happened? I asked, is it the electrician?" I asked. "Yes!" Carlos replied,

"Did you see that bolt of lightning? it struck him, and he is dead. Quick! Come down with me and see for yourself." Charlotte and I followed Carlos to the basement.

The electric box was still on fire, and not having a fire extinguisher, Carlos decided to leave it burning. We had to rely on the torch to see, that is when we saw the electrician lying flat on his back on the floor motionless.

"Quick! check whether he is breathing," Charlotte said to me.

I knelt down to check whether he was breathing, and thank God he was, his pulse was faint, but at least he was alive. "Wake up! wake up!" I shouted to him but he did not respond.

None of us even knew his name. I shook him several times, that is when he opened his eyes. "Where am I? what am I doing here? and who are you?" he asked.

He started convulsing, and foaming from his mouth. "Charlotte go home quick and phone for an ambulance,"

I shouted.

She dashed out while I attended to the electrician, and Carlos just stood there in awe. I wiped the foam off his mouth using the sleeve of his blue sweater which he was wearing. Then slugs came out of his mouth, I did not react at all, with all the phenomena's that had been happening, nothing shocked me anymore. At least he was still alive.

"Are you alright Carlos!" I shouted to a shaken Carlos. "I am fine Suzanna, you just look after him," he responded.

Sophia had heard Carlos shouting for help, she panicked then immediately came downstairs and into the basement. "Are you alright in there?" she shouted before opening the basement door.

"I heard screams," she said.

She walked in, and saw the electrician lying on the floor. "What happened? and where is Charlotte?" she panted. "He got electrocuted but he is fine, and Charlotte has gone home to phone for an ambulance. If we are lucky, dad might be home, and come to our aid," I replied.

"Is that slugs coming out of his mouth?" Sophia asked.

Even Sophia wasn't petrified seeing the slugs coming out of his mouth, I bet like me and Charlotte she was getting used to seeing things unusual.

"I have seen those slugs before! I have seen them before!" Carlos yelled.

"Remember the night Audrey took ill, the night she was taken to hospital, slugs like those came out of her mouth as well. What does that mean?" he asked.

"I don't know Carlos, just stay calm till help arrives," I replied.

The electrician sat up, vomiting more and more slugs, he was losing colour off his face appearing more more grey. His pulse was very faint.

"Go get a blanket for him Sophia, he getting cold," I shouted.

Sophia quickly dashed back upstairs to Carlos' bedroom, and came back with a thick hand knitted blanket. We covered him up, then Sophia ran to Bramwells for help. Dad was relaxing in the drawing room reading his newspaper.

When she got there, she explained everything to him. Before long Sophia and dad turned up.

"What is going on? the ambulance is on its way," he said. "Dad I am sure Sophia has explained things to you and I don't have to repeat it, I think it is happening again," I replied.

"What's happening again?" Carlos asked.

"Never mind Carlos, it is best you don't know, you just think of yourself, your health and Audrey, and we will deal with the rest," dad reassured.

"Alright Ed, you and your family have been so good to me Audrey, and I trust that you know what you are doing," he replied.

"How is the electrician?" dad asked.

"Well, he is breathing, and the ambulance is going to be here soon, at least they can take over. "Those slugs! I have seen them before! from Audrey," dad exclaimed.

"Yeah dad, we know, Carlos mentioned the same thing, I think everything happening to us and Carlos and Audrey are all interlinked," I responded.

"Where are those paramedics? He could die here, right in front of our eyes," yelled Sophia.

There was a knock on the door.

"I take it it's them, I will get the door," Sophia muttered.

She went upstairs, answered the door, and it was the paramedics.

"This is the second time in one week that we are responding to an emergency at this address," one paramedic said as they walked in through the door.

By then dad was at the door as well.

"I know, I feel like a nuisance, it was me who called you the last time, and I called you again today, my apologies," dad said.

He explained to them what had happened. They attended to the electrician, whom by then we didn't even know his name. They put him on oxygen, then onto the stretcher and had to take him to the hospital, just like they did with Audrey, except this time, none of us accompanied him to the hospital. When they yanked him into the ambulance, he was still vomiting slugs. After he was gone, dad set on to look for the slugs in the basement, but we couldn't see any, they had all disappeared. Dad even pulled out the wine shelves, but they were not there, they had simply vanished into thin air. "I wonder what them paramedics are going to make of them slugs? perhaps they will simply overlook it, just like they did with Audrey," dad commented. Carlos was still standing there in shock motionless, like a door nail,

What was that all about?

"The guy got electrocuted without even touching the electric box, I saw it with my own eyes," Carlos expressed.

"I know Carlos," dad replied,

"These are the phenomena's in which we are all trying to make sense of Carlos, let us worry about all that, okay," dad replied.

Carlos appeared a little bit lost but he kept nodding, agreeing with whatever dad was saying. "The girls will stay with you Carlos but now I better go home to check on Jane, then I will come back later on and stay with you while the girls visit Audrey, as arranged yesterday. Charlotte and Suzanna will go to the hospital later, while Sophia rests at home with her mother," dad stated.

"Whatever you say Ed, you know best," Carlos replied. Poor Carlos was in hysterics, his hands and legs shaking uncontrollably, partly from early signs of parkinsons disease and partly from fear.

# CHAPTER 13

When dad got home, he was relieved to find mum okay, she was smiling away.

He stayed home till about 5.30pm, that is when he came to pick Charlotte, Sophia and I to visit Audrey while mum stayed with Carlos. After visiting Audrey dad dropped me and Charlotte at Carlos' to spend the night as arranged. He picked mum up, and Sophia went home with them.

We had a peaceful night, Charlotte and I woke up first, we were up by about 7.30am, Charlotte made breakfast for Carlos, then we went home, Dad or mum or any one of the family was going to drop by later to keep an eye on him. Charlotte and started planning about our day. Our mission was to go to the prison and visit Melvin, mum and dad did not know about our plan. The earliest visiting time at the prison was 8.30am, so it gave us enough time to get washed and ready to go about 8.00am which meant Sophia and dad will just be up to get ready to go to their prospective jobs. By the time they left for work, Charlotte and I were already gone. We had phoned a taxi to pick us up for 8.00am, and we got to the prison exactly 8.30am when they allowed the prisoners to have visitors. Melvin was shocked to hear that he had visitors that early; his parents had visited him daily without failure, but only in the afternoon. He was petrified to see us.

"And what the hell are you doing here?" he asked in a sly manner when he saw us.

"We have brought you some fruit and lunch," Charlotte replied.

Charlotte and I had stolen some grapes, apples and strawberries from home, and we also stole some of mum's home made sausage rolls, which had taken the trouble to make the day before. That accompanied with some green leaf salad, it was an appetising lunch no one could resist. Alongside the sausage rolls was also pork pies, which was mum's speciality for eternity. The prison guards allowed him time with us, we were led off to some seclusive little garden, part of the prison grounds of cause.

"If you share some of what you have got in that basket, we will give you an extra hour with your friends," the prison guards said to Melvin.

He shared his lunch with them, and they could not get over, how wonderful the pies tasted and the pork pies.

"Two extra hours, we give you," said the bossy guard, "but you have got to behave, or else we incarcerate you." "I will behave, "Melvin responded nervously.

Prison life seemed tough for Melvin, it seemed to have humbled him a lot, as it was based on a form of good behaviour reward system, which he was never used to at all. We went to the secluded garden, even that privilege had to be earned, and Melvin had earned it through the sausage rolls and pork pies. We sat down on some old wooden benches, that is when Charlotte felt she had to confront him. Since it was still early in the morning, Melvin had had his prison breakfast, which was porridge, and no doubt he wasn't looking forward to the stodgy lunch neither, he chose to keep the lunch which we had brought for him for later. We managed to get some free coffees from the kind guards, whom we had managed to bribe with mum's pies. We sat there on them old benches drinking coffee, even Melvin had one, that is when Charlotte decided to cut the chase and question him why he broke into our home. To begin with Melvin tried denying everything, but after a while of interrogation from Charlotte and me, he decided to come out clean. It was only when Charlotte said,

"We have the powers to set you free," that is when he chose to collaborate.

"I will tell you whatever you want to hear, as long as you get me out of here. Vicar Simms let me down, big time, and now I know he is not a friend, he is just out there to serve his own purpose," he replied.

"I miss my family," Melvin continued.

"And I will do anything to be back with them again." "I miss my mum's cooking, the smell of my home and everything else, ask me anything and I will tell you, as long as you promise to get me out of here," he pleaded.

I looked at Charlotte, and we both concluded that he was genuine.

"It was vicar Simms who got me to do it! he got me to break into your home, he told me that the whole town depended on your family destruction, and that the book of life that made it all possible was in your home. He said to me that, if I retrieve the book and give it to him, my family will be rewarded in money, power and eternal life," he confessed.

"However he advised me that, either the book is in your home, or Carlos'. He had specifically that I had to obtain the book, either from your home or Audrey's, but I never got round to going to Audrey's, your dad caught me in the act, and that is why I am here."

Charlotte and I were puzzled, we looked at each other then simultaneously shook our heads. "Why didn't you tell the police about that?" I questioned him.

He shook his head then replied,

"I never thought about that, besides Simms had threatened me that if I ever spoke to anybody about it, he will make sure that my family would be banished from the town for ever. My father worked so hard to be where he is today, the thought of him destroyed would have killed me. If I knew that I was going to end up alone in prison, I would never have listened to that Simms. He has never been to visit me in prison!" Melvin cried.

"I doubt, he is a true Christian? you should always be careful, what so called man of faith you choose to follow?" I proclaimed.

"I couldn't!" Melvin exclaimed.

"He threatened me by saying that my parents are part of the whole thing, and that they are deeply interwoven with the town secret, and that they want it to happen."

"What is going to happen?" I questioned him intently. "Is my family in danger! is it Melvin!?" Charlotte shouted.

Melvin looked around helplessly, "I am afraid so," he replied.

"It is only through your deaths that the new cycle begins, so Simms said. He said if I didn't participate, it will be my family instead that will perish, and of cause I didn't want that to happen to my family. Charlotte got up from the bench and punched Melvin in the face, "Rather my family hey! is that good enough for you!" she shouted.

The prison guards were watching us, after Charlotte punched Melvin, they came immediately, one prison guard said,

"Enough! it is time you go now!".

We were not done with Melvin, the guards escorted us out.

"What about SAC Melvin! what does it mean!?" Charlotte shouted as the guards forced us out.

"I will tell you about it next time! but be careful!" he shouted back.

The guards were forcing him back to his cell. Charlotte and I were thrown out of the prison just like that, and we wondered whether we were ever going to be welcome again as Melvin's visitors. "What's going to happen to Melvin?" I questioned Charlotte as we made our way out of the prison.

I anticipated that vicar Simms would soon know that we had been there, and he would punish Melvin for talking to us. We left about 11.30am, and got back home about 12.15pm, dad was at work, and so was Sophia, and mum was in bed resting from all the escapades, since she was a faint hearted one, so it wasn't surprising to us. Charlotte and I, between the two of us decided to make some lunch for the three of us. We woke mum up when we were done; she was delighted to have some company.

"Perhaps, I don't have to feel afraid anymore alone in this house, now I sleep in order to shadow the fears," she said.

"Where have you been anyway, I was feeling pretty scared here all by myself," she questioned. "Oh! nowhere in particular except at Audrey's," I replied.

Charlotte and I had decided prior to getting home that we were not going to tell her about our visit to the prison.

"But I called Audrey and Carlos to find out whether you were there, and they said you were not there, I say! that old couple must be going senile or something! Jesus Christ! what we have got to put up with. I bet they can't even tie their shoe laces up without any help, I keep telling your father not to get involved with them two old folks," she said.

"Never mind mum, we are here now," Charlotte said.

We had our lunch, and as we sat at the table mum seemed to be normal again. She never coped with being alone in the cottage, it made her a nervous wreck, I think that is why she enjoyed Charlotte and I to be be there always; but now with Charlotte seeming to be pairing off nicely with doctor Edelbert, she could be soon gone, married to him of cause, and that will mean only I left with her all the time; I couldn't handle that. If Charlotte were to leave I will have to leave as well. I had to be forced to find love somewhere as well, and disappear from Bramwells as well, and perhaps Melvin wasn't such a bad match for Sophia, takeaway the town doctor, and maybe she should settle for him and escape Bramwells. I thought of influencing Sophia to visit Melvin in prison, if they get on, they might marry and run away as far as possible from the town and Bramwells and live happily ever after without the drama and divisions created by the town. We finished our lunch, hung around with mum for about an hour or so just to make her confident again, then we left for Audrey's, we still needed to get the book from her, provided she had got it off Carlos. When we got to Audrey's, Carlos was in the garden, the front door was open so we let ourselves in. Audrey was sat on one of the recliners motionless, the blood veins throughout her body were sticking out, darkened in colour, the dark colour had run through from the black book she was clutching.

"Audrey! Audrey!" I shouted, but there was no response. I shook her and shook her, but still there was no response, she appeared as if she was as stiff as a board. Charlotte checked her pulse, she had a weak pulse and she was breathing shallowly. "Quick Charlotte! do you have one of those silver coins which we got from Father Francis!

"I shouted.

Luckily Charlotte had one in her pocket, she had decided to move around with one wherever she was going to go.

"Place it on her forehead just like Father Francis said!" I yelled.

So Charlotte got the coin from her pocket, placed it on Audrey's forehead, and we waited. After a few seconds, Audrey revived, and she was back to her old self, so Charlotte grabbed the book from her and she put it her bag.

"Audrey! you shouldn't play with things like that, not at your age anyway, you know how dangerous this book is," Charlotte said to her.

Carlos was in oblivion, he was still working away in his garden pruning some hedge, we chose not to arouse him.

"I managed to take the book from Carlos," Audrey whispered, she appeared worn out and tired.

"I confronted him last night about the book, and it turned out he had hid from you inside the mattress, he meant no harm by it, he thought he was protecting you. It was till I told him of your visit to Father Francis, he opened up, and even wore the rosary beads you gave us," she stated. "That book is dangerous," I said to her.

"From now on we keep the book till we give it to Father Francis," I continued.

Audrey accepted that,

"I was going to give it to you anyway, I felt it belonged to you," she sobbed.

After Charlotte used the silver coin she retained it back in her pocket, now we trusted Father Francis, and we couldn't wait for his arrival in a few days to end all this.

"Do you know anything else Audrey?" Charlotte questioned.

Audrey looked left and right, appeared a bit confused then she replied.

"Apart from what I have already told you, there is nothing else, and don't ask about SAC because I don't know what it means. I spent the whole night going through that black book, to see if there was anything about SAC, but I couldn't find anything. Now I feel I have done my best to try and protect your family, and if God was to take me today, I will go with a clear conscience," she said.

"Don't worry about anything Audrey, none of this is your fault nor Carlos' just leave everything with us," I reassured.

After getting the book, and now that Audrey was alright, Charlotte and I didn't stay long at Audrey's, Carlos and her were alright and so we didn't need feel bad at all for leaving early.

"We have got to go Audrey!" Charlotte said.

"We have got a lot a lot of things to take care of at home," Charlotte apologised as we left.

At least we had the book finally and were looking forward to some closure of all these paranormal activities. When we got home Charlotte and I couldn't wait for Sophia to come back from work and explain to her what was going on with Melvin, at least he deserved a bit of empathy. By that time it was about 5.30pm, dad walked in first from work, followed by Sophia, both of them in good spirits, work seemed to have shadowed them from the escapades of Bramwell cottage. Mum was in the kitchen still fiddling away to calm her nerves.

"I am so glad to see you back," she said to Charlotte and me when we stepped in the kitchen. Dad walked in the kitchen, followed by Sophia, he expected a cup of tea from mum.

"I will make everybody a cup of tea," mum expressed in a passive manner.

"What have you girls been up to?" dad asked me and Charlotte.

He put his briefcase down, reached out for his cup of tea and grinned,

"I am sure you have been up to no good," he cried. "My day was good," Sophia interrupted.

Charlotte and I decided to tell them, what we had been up to. We talked about going to the prison, and about what we talked about with Audrey, and what we learnt from her and the book that we had in our possession. Mum and dad were shocked naturally, and so was Sophia, there she was thinking Melvin, this dark character, and all the while he was a victim himself just like us. She felt deep compassion and love for him.

"I must have misunderstood him," she thought to herself.

"We feel sorry for Melvin, it is not his fault," Charlotte said to Sophia.

"Perhaps you should visit him in prison, and he will tell you more than he has told us," I suggested.

That day was Friday, and Sophia did not work Saturday just like dad.

"I will visit him tomorrow in prison, may be dad can come with me," she stated.

"Of cause! I will come with you, I am just as curious as all of you are," dad replied.

"I would like you to, dad," she responded, "after all, I don't think at that prison, they would want to see Charlotte and Suzanna again."

Mum simply smiled then shouted,

"I have made shepherd's pie and green beans for dinner, it is all ready now."

Dad was getting concerned about Audrey and Carlos. "I think before we eat, I am going to nip over to Carlos',

I won't be long, I just want to know that they are alright," he said.

He grabbed his coat, put it on and walked out to Carlos'. He was back in no time, "They are alright there, when I walked in they were having their supper, so I did not want to stay. Audrey seems to be in good spirits since she left the hospital," dad said. We all sat at the table had dinner and enjoyed mum's special shepherd's pie, we did not talk any more about the strange phenomena going on within the cottage.

After dinner we went to bed, but before, Charlotte and I went to Sophia's room and talked more about Melvin.

Was she really going to visit him in prison the following dad?

"Dad promised that he will go with me to the prison!" Sophia said.

"So I trust that he will," she exclaimed. "Melvin might tell you more Sophia," I sighed,
"ask him what SAC means, none of us know and neither does Audrey."
"I surely will, I want this crap ended just like you do, trust me," she replied.
"So that's sorted then, tomorrow!" Charlotte responded. We left Sophia's room, and Charlotte and I felt confident. "We just have to remind her to take the silver coins with her in the morning," I said to Charlotte.
"And don't forget, you have got your date with doctor Edelbert as well," I added before closing my bedroom door behind Charlotte.

The house was quiet for a while, I thought everybody was asleep till I heard mum talking to dad then walking about fiddling as usual in the kitchen trying to calm her nerves. She couldn't sleep, thereby keeping dad awake, I barely slept as a result. All I could hear was saucepans rattling in the kitchen. Come morning, I was exhausted, so was dad, but lucky enough he wasn't going in to work and neither was Sophia. She and dad were going to going to visit Melvin in prison that morning, while Charlotte had a date with Matthew. I dreaded the thought of me being left alone with mum, anyhow Charlotte's date was in the evening, hopefully by then Sophia would have been back from the prison. I did not go downstairs for breakfast, but I heard Sophia and dad up about 8am getting ready to go to the prison. They left the house quietly and managed not to wake mum nor Sophia. I sat up in bed wondering what was going to happen at the prison, no doubt Melvin would not want to see neither dad nor Sophia, he would be too ashamed. So I decided to wake Charlotte up and talk to her about it. We talked and talked for ages anticipating all sorts of possibilities. Mum then was fast asleep, the dawn of day seemed to comfort her, and that was the only time she could sleep comfortably. Dad and Sophia got to the prison, they asked at the reception to see Melvin. The receptionist appeared out of all sorts, she scratched her head, paced up and down for a while without saying a word. Dad looked at Sophia in bemusement, he shook his head then whispered to Sophia,

"What is going on? Something is up?" Sophia simply nodded her head,

"Just calm down dad, we will find out in a minute," she whispered back.

The receptionist smiled at them then responded,

"I will just get my supervisor to talk to you. Are you family?" she asked.

"No we are not, but we are friends," dad replied.

She nipped out and came back with the supervisor, he was a tall man, of stocky built, clean shaven with tattoos covering his arms. He was dressed in prison guard uniform, navy blue trousers and short sleeved shirt. He spoke with a very deep voice, his whole persona was intimidating.

"Well are you family of Melvin, because at the moment we are only talking to his family only," he asked.

He spoke while sizing dad up and down and definitely looked at me in a suspicious manner.

"And who are you!" he asked me while staring at me up and down. All of sudden dad and I felt unwelcome, "Perhaps we should leave dad?" she whispered.

Dad held her hand tight, "We are not going anyway, till we speak to Melvin," he reassured.

"Just stand behind me," he added.

"I am his girlfriend, is that good enough?" she responded. The prison guard wore a badge, and his name was John. John rubbed his face then replied, "That is okay, I believe you. There has been an incident, Melvin is dead. He was found early this morning dead in his cell. The police are treating the incident with suspicion, and there is an investigation. I understand your daughters visited him yesterday?" he asked dad.

"Afterwards a priest who calls himself vicar Simms visited him. As far as we know, this vicar Simms was the last person to talk to him before he was found dead," he added. "Right now we are trying to contact his family, do you know anything at all that might have caused his death?"

John said.

"No we don't," dad replied, "but I am sure you know that Melvin broke into my home a while ago, and that is the reason why he was here," dad added.

"When do you think you will know, what happened to him?" dad asked.

"Well, that depends on a lot of things, like the police investigation and post mortem of cause," he replied.

"I guess there is no reason for us to hang around any longer," dad replied.

"Before you go leave your phone number and address, then we will contact you with any details that we find."

Dad left him with the contact details, and they left. "What a shame about Melvin," Sophia said to dad as they left the prison.

On the way back home, they discussed Melvin. "Maybe vicar Simms did something to him, in order to silence him. He must have known that Charlotte and Suzanna had visited him," dad said.

"I have always known that vicar Simms is not to be trusted," Sophia added.

They got home within the hour of them leaving, Charlotte, mum and I were shocked to learn of Melvin's death. We discussed the possibilities of what could have accumulated to his death, and we all came to an agreement that it had something to do with the cult.

"I am going to confront that vicar Simms," dad expressed.

"Sometimes it is better to grab the bull by its horns, or hear it from the horses mouth, than wonder," dad exclaimed.

I am going to his place this afternoon and confront him," he added.

"Perhaps I should come with you, you know you can't go there alone, it is not safe," mum suggested.

"Very well! You come with me," dad replied, "but it has got to be this afternoon."

We discussed Melvin for the rest of the morning, and come afternoon doctor Adelbert came to pick Charlotte up for their date. He knocked at the door, and dad answered, he hardly said a word to him before calling Charlotte who had been busy grooming herself. By then it was only a couple of days left before Father Francis would turn up for the exorcism of Bramwells. Charlotte went on her date, while mum and dad went to vicar Simms to confront him about Melvin and also the cult. Doctor Edelbert picked Charlotte up around 2pm, I must say he appeared scared even driving through Bramwells.

'What have I got myself into?' he questioned himself as he drove through the cottage.

Charlotte was ready, and off she went.

"Do you want to come to my place?" he asked her, "or we could go elsewhere?" he said.

"Your place would be fine, I want to see where you live," Charlotte replied; so they went to his place.

# CHAPTER 14

Edelbert lived in an apartment in town, it was very well decorated, neutral colours on the walls, and he lived a very minimalistic life. There was no clutter in the apartment, everything was in its place, and there was very little furniture. It was a one bed apartment, with a very neat closet holding all his clothings, neatly ironed and hanging in the closet.

"You live very well," Charlotte said to him.

"I try to, clutter breeds negative energies and results in a clouded mind," he replied.

"I believe in a positive flow of air and energy and clutter can hinder that. The way you live reflects your whole life what it is about, so I believe anyway," he added.

"I understand you," Charlotte replied as she sat down on one of the fine settees in the lounge. "I hope your parents are going to be fine, visiting vicar Simms, everybody knows him in town including the hospital; he is like a feared man. I am in your life now and I am not going to walk away from you, I want you to be safe, so that you and I can have a life together," he exclaimed.

"I know!" Charlotte responded.

"I want to see this through, Father Francis is coming in two days time and hopefully all the trouble will stop after the exorcism. I am going to be there with you when he does the exorcism," Edelbert expressed.

"I would like you to be, then I can feel safe," she responded.

There was no doubt about it, Charlotte felt very safe with Matthew, even though she never spoke of it, we all knew that, he was becoming her rock. After being at Matthew's Charlotte came back home feeling a bit humbled, Matthew was going to stick with her to the very end, she felt what true commitment was all about. He never asked anything off her, except her love and affection.

"I will be here tomorrow when Father Francis comes," he shouted at her as he waved goodbye to her at Bramwells. "No doubt, it will be an adventure," she smirked then said goodbye to him.

When she came home, we were all sat in the kitchen wondering about the happenings of tomorrow when Father Francis come. Dad and Sophia spoke of their experience at the prison and were so eager to share with the rest of the family of Melvin's predicament. mum and dad had been to vicar Simms, they had got there and knocked and knocked but never got no reply, so they returned feeling empty.

"Never mind Jane, I am sure we will learn more from Father Francis when he comes tomorrow right!" dad said.

Supper that night was dull, we had boiled potatoes, fried sausages and some boiled greens. mum didn't feel cooking so she opted for the easiest solution. We all sat there munching on dry sausages, dry potatoes and boiled mixed vegetables. We ate because we were hungry, we hardly spoke at the dinner table, and soon after dinner, we all went to bed respectively anticipating of Father Francis visit.

# CHAPTER 15

Following day, we were all up early with anticipation of what the day will bring.

"What time did he say he is going to be here?" mum asked.

It was about 7am, we were all up, dad and Sophia had booked days off work, this was more important than work, we had decided. Charlotte and I were still in our pyjamas when we came downstairs.

"He said about 9 o'clock Charlotte replied, so we have got 2 hours to kill".

We had our breakfast which was oats porridge that mum had prepared, and thereafter we went to get changed. Charlotte was very hesitant, while I was preparing myself, I got the silver coins that Father Francis had given to us, and equipped myself with the rosary beads, I wore them around my neck and had Audrey's black book ready so that I could give it to him the minute he walked in. I wanted to ask him about the meaning of SAC. The next two hours was followed by silence, that is when Matthew Edelbert arrived, waiting for Father Francis just like the rest of us.

"Perhaps we should go get Audrey and Carlos," Charlotte suggested, "because we wouldn't want whatever it is, to go to them, after it has been exorcised from here," she continued. "Wise idea!" dad replied, "I will go and fetch them now." Dad being dressed all ready and waiting, nipped off to Carlos', and before long he was back with them two. Audrey and Carlos were still in their night clothes. They both felt confident in what dad was doing, so they didn't question him at all. Melvin was highly anxious, he had brought with him a couple of silver coins which Sophia had given him the night before. Father Francis arrived around half past nine, he blamed the traffic for his delay.

"So are you ready for the exorcism?" he exclaimed. "Before you begin father," Sophia expressed, "did you find out anything or the meaning of SAC father?" Father Francis took a big sigh, then replied,

"SAC was a sacrificial name used back in the time of father Carlos for human sacrifices chosen by the cult. It means Sacrificial Agents Chosen."

"So does it mean we are the chosen sacrifice?" Charlotte asked.

"What about me?" Edelbert asked.

"Well! normally it is the chosen family, that is appropriate, but we have to go to the Abbey before performing the exorcism, we need to cleanse the place, and find the dagger with that inscription. When we find the dagger, we are to burn it with the silver coins till it becomes molten rock, then we will weaken the spirit and displace its powers, but we have to do this before nightfall, because the spirit is more powerful at night," he added.

"We have got some of your silver coins, we could use those," dad exclaimed.

"Don't worry, I have got enough with me, we better not waste time let's go there now," Father Francis replied.

We got the black book, wore our rosaries and we headed towards the Abbey. Father Francis brought his exorcism bible with him, it was a few minutes walk away from Bramwells. When we got to the Abbey, we were shocked to see vicar Simms already there grinning away.

"Whatever you are going to try and do, it is not going to work, because this is a binding covenant," he said.

"It will work," Father Francis replied.

"Then I shall have the great pleasure of watching," vicar Simms responded.

He sat in one corner of the Abbey observing carefully, he lit his cigar and sat back to watch. Father Francis led us to the alter, then he started praying, he got his holy water, and sprinkled it round the alter. The minute he did that, we heard loud sounds, like mourning sounds echoing around the Abbey. Shadows of people appeared all around the Abbey and appeared to be chasing each other. Father Carlos appeared dressed in all red, holding a dagger and he went straight for vicar Simms. He stabbed him through the heart,

"You betrayed me Simms!" he shouted in a ghostly manner."

Simms fell to the ground, and was bleeding from the head, his blood was black in colour.

"I only wanted to serve you master, that is all!" he shouted as he got up, only to fall again, then he died. Father Francis then threw the silver coins around the alter, a grand hole formed at the centre, and fire was burning, it appeared like hell, with all these dead souls wailing. Father Carlos rushed for the hole so that he could disappear in it, but Father Francis stopped him. He tripped him then grabbed the knife from him just before he jumped in the fire.

"We have got the knife! We have got the knife!" Father Francis shouted.

Father Carlos disappeared in the furnace alongside the shadowy figures, then the hole closed again leaving a clean surface.

"Now we have got rid of father Carlos, it will be easy to finish the ritual. We have got to get back and burn the black books together with the dagger, but we have to molten the dagger first, hurry now! because we have got to finish the ritual before midnight," Father Francis said.

So we left the Abbey swiftly, and Edelbert followed behind, when we got to Bramwell, Father Francis pointed the dagger out and used it as a guide to find out where the right place was to finish the ritual. He went through all the rooms, till he got to bathroom, that is when the dagger pointed down wards at the drainage chamber.

"This is the place!" Father Francis shouted.

"Bring me some coal, a barrel or a rubbish bin lid, some kerosene and matchstick. This is where we have to melt the dagger together with silver coins."

Dad hurried downstairs to the garage, and in no time he came back holding a rubbish bin lid, some coal, kerosene and matchsticks.

"Let's all form a circle of protection, remember, this is very dangerous! If not handled well, it can kill the whole lot of us; so pay attention and follow instructions," Father Francis exclaimed.

We all joined hands, including Audrey and Carlos, and Edelbert. Father Francis stood in the middle, read a few sentences from his catholic bible of exorcism. He put the two black books on the rubbish bin lid, poured a lot of coal on top, poured the kerosene and then placed placed the dagger on top, accompanied by the silver coins, then he lit the match. The contents went on fire instantly, giving off a nasty whiff; the flames went in bright red colour.

"Whatever you do, keep your eyes closed, and don't look into the flames, because if you do the unclean spirit will come into you, and then we will have to start the whole process again; Father Carlos will be back, so as Simms and the rest of the unclean spirits. So don't open your eyes till I tell you to, do you understand Audrey and Carlos, and the rest of you,?" Father Francis shouted.

"Yes we do," we all replied.

The dagger was moulting, and so screeches started coming out of the fire, it sounded like weeping souls. It scared Carlos so bad that he opened his eyes, screamed, and started running out of the bathroom and out of Bramwells. Audrey was the next one to open her eyes after being aroused by Carlos' screams. Her body then went into flames, only leaving a statue of burnt coal and ash.

"Keep focused! Or else we will all die!" Father Francis shouted, "and do not look at the flames."

Eventually the dagger and the coins melted, and the screeching stopped.

"It is over now!, you can open your eyes!," Father Francis shouted.

We all opened our eyes to the horror of seeing Audrey body turn into burnt coal and ash; she was like a statue made out of burnt coal.

"What happened to Audrey!? Mum screamed; and where is Carlos?" she questioned some more.

"Carlos panicked during the ritual, and he ran away, and so Audrey panicked, opened her eyes and stared at the flames, that is why she got attacked," Father Francis replied. Charlotte, Sophia and I were dumbstruck, none of us was sure that the ordeal was over, there was something there,

that gave us a feeling that it wasn't over. "So what does that mean?" asked dad. "Is it over?" mum yelled.

Father Francis paced up and down, scratched his head, then replied,

"I don't know! if the ritual is unsuccessful, it means that it is not over yet. It might mean that father Carlos is not destroyed, perhaps vicar Simms as well. There is also the danger that they will return much more powerful than before."

By then it was midnight, Father Francis decided to reside, and leave the the rest for the following day. So he was going to spend the night at Bramwells', by that he was hoping to trigger something out of the ordinary to happen there. We went home, Dr Edelbert decided to spend the the night at Bramwells as well, joined together with Carlos our neighbour. Nothing got us over Audrey's demise, but Father Francis advised us not to contact the local police, because he did not know how far deep this thing went within the local community.

"I advise you not to involve the police, especially in this early stage of exorcism, for all you know, it has pernetrated through their system," he said.

In as much as Carlos lamented, so did we all, over Audrey's death, but it was a no! no!, delving with local police. So we all had to swallow it hard, and accept the fact that we couldn't afford any more deaths happenings. Carlos was too scared to spent the night alone, so he decided to sleep at Bramwells, sharing a room with Father Francis; while Edelbert was excused by mum and dad from sharing a room with Charlotte, it seemed like none of morality mattered any more for them, except life itself. Carlos was too scared to give a moments thought about grieving for Audrey, so he lay there in complecent wondering about Audrey's death. We all slept well at Bramwells, following morning was eventful; mum made breakfast for the whole of us, Father Francis was the first one up, he was saying prayers privately in the bathroom where he felt the evil spirits where coming from. It was 7.30am, mum was the first one up, besides Father Francis who was lost in prayer, she was making cooked breakfast, she made tonnes of bacon, egg, mushroom and et-cetera. Father Francis had been up since 6am praying.

"I believe a good breakfast would do everybody good," she said to him.

Father Francis stayed close to his cricifix, then replied, "I agree with you, a good breakfast would fix us all, to face another day."

He got his holy water, grabbed his exorcism bible together with his rosarey beads, then retreated up to the main bathroom where he felt the evil was coming from.

He knelt down and started reciting the Lords prayer, he opened the little bottle of holy water, then sprinkled it in the bathroom; he then opened his bible of exorcism and started reading from it. The minute he started reading from the exorcism bible, black shadows started from everywhere in the bathroom, they were spinning round and round. Then he started hearing these hissing sounds, they so loud and profound in his ears that he couldn't function any more. He covered his ears, but it didn't help at all, it sounded like very loud whispers that he couldn't control. He ran for the door, but the door locked on him, and he couldn't open it. A deep vault of lave opened itself in the middle of the bathroom, it was like hell opening its gateway, but he wasn't going to be sucked in it, not if he can help it. He clutched his bible and carried on reading from it; he heard the voice of vicar Simms, Audrey's and father Carlos', all were calling on him to join them. Father Francis closed his eyes, shut his self from them, that is when he got absorbed in the furnace and disappeared in the furnace.

By then mum had finished preparing breakfast, then called everybody down to eat, Carlos came down first, followed by Dr Edelbert, then dad, Charlotte, Sophia and I. One person was missing at the dinner table, and it was Father Francis.

"Why don't you go up Charlotte, and get Father Francis!" mum shouted.

Everybody was ready for an early breakfast, all sat at the dinner table, so Charlotte got up swiftly and ran upstairs.

"Father Francis! Father Francis! It's breakfast time!" she shouted continually, but there was no reply.

"Father Francis!" she shouted some more, but this time she sounded quaite anxiously; but still there was no reply.

So Charlotte came running back downstairs anxiously, "He is not there!" she shouted.

"Maybe, he ran away in the middle of the night," she exclaimed.

"He wouldn't do that, he is not the type to do that!" mum responded.

"Go find him and tell him, breakfast is ready. Maybe he is in the garden, or something."

Before long we were all looking for him with a fine toothed comb. Carlos, bless him, still grieving for Audrey, got Dr Edelbert and were searching in the garden, while the rest of us searched in the cottage.

"Father Francis! Father Francis!" Carlos shouted in the garden, but there was no response.

He even dragged Dr Edelbert to his garden next door, searching; but to no use. We searched in the cottage, and unfortunately, he was nowhere to be seen. We decided to have breakfast without him.

"He will show up at some point," mum said reassuringly.

I must say, we were all scared, but managed to swallow that breakfast with some fack confidence.

"He will show up," Carlos said hesitantly.

"Maybe he had to nip off to get something from his parish, and he will back," dad instigated, while we swallowed hard on our breakfast.

"I think it's over now, maybe that is why he decided to leave," Sophia exclaimed with hesitation. "Yeh! You are right there," we all responded.

But deep inside, all of us feared the worst, it wasn't over, by any means. We finished our breakfast in false glee, but then dad went to the bathroom, where he felt deep suspicions of. He looked round the bathroom, searching for some clues, but there was none to be found. He came back downstairs scratching his head, as he alwalys did when he was worried about something.

"What am I going to explain to my children when they ask about their mother?" Carlos exclaimed.

Dad paced up and down, thinking, and scratching his head as usual; he thought of a plan.

"Don't tell them anything yet, till we all feel this thing is over. I am sure it is going to take a few more days, till we figure out," he responded.

"It is okay Ed! I trust you, whatever you say," Carlos replied. He was back being the vulnerable person that he had always been, in front of patronising mum and dad; he was back to being helpless in front of them. According to Carlos, they always had the answer to everything, and all the while he had allowed them to patronise him and Audrey.

Carlos grew an instant liking to Edelbert, so he decided to take him to his cottage after breakfast, none of us objected, so they walked to Carlos' while he fed him stories about him and Audrey. They got to the cottage, and Carlos showed him round the cottage, and even showed him his proud possession, his garden filled with roses. Dr Edelbert immediately fell for Carlos' charm. It was as if, Carlos felt safer with Edelbert than my own family, that had always been there for him and Audrey. He was less afraid, in the company of Edelbert, Dr Edelbert spoke of Audrey's ordeal while in hospital, and how he found it so bizarre. They went through the library, in Carlos' cottage, the after an exhausting two hours, they came back to Bramwells. Mum made some tea, which she served with some home made cookies. By then we still hadn't heard from Father Francis; it was only till finishing the tea, we saw Father Francis walking down the drive. He looked worn out, staggering from left to right, as if he were a drunken man. His whole body was covered in dust; he knocked at the door, as if he were a desperate beggar.

"We thought he had abandoned us!" mum screeched.

She quickly opened the door for him, and appeared so helpless to try and make things right for him, because of the state that he was in.

"Quickly grab a towel and a bowl of warm water!" she shouted at Charlotte.

Dad was perplexed, but weren't we all.

"Father Francis! Where have you been?" he questioned several times.

He collapsed in mum's arms, the minute he walked in, he was gasping for breathe.

"You don't want to know where I have been! It is far from over!" he gasped before passing out on the couch in the living room.

By then Charlotte was back downstairs with a bowl of warm water, a flannel and a bath towel. Dad carefully laid him on the couch, while mum started washing his face, hands and feet. I rushed to the kitchen and fetched a glass of water with a straw in it.

"Here try and get him to sip some water," I suggested to mum.

After washing him and covering him with a blanket, the fire was roaring on in the living room; Father Francis started regaining consciousness, and was sipping on the water.

"What happened?" dad exclaimed.

Carlos and Dr Edelbert just stared on, and then after a while the pair of them disappeared in the garden for a quiete word.

"Carlos seems to be quiete estranged from us, and appears to be bonding more with Carlos," Sophia whispered in my ear.

"Don't you find that a bit strange," she added.

I didn't think much of it, given mum and dad's patronising nature towards him, it didn't surprise me at all, maybe now he had found somebody that he could feel comfortable with. Carlos grabbed Edelberts hand as he dragged him out to the garden.

"I have always known that something like this was going to happen," Carlos said.

"I had no idea when, but I knew it will happen at some point; I loved Audrey, and I had sworn to protect her at all times," he added.

"You are a nice man Edelbert, my suggestion to you, is walk away now, you don't know what you are getting yourself involved in," he continued.

Edelbert looked confused, he stared at Carlos up and down in bewilderment. "You are not suggesting I walk away from Charlotte, are you? I will protect her from whatever, just like you felt protection over Audrey," he replied.

Edelbert covered his mouth with his left hand in awe. "What do you know about all this Carlos? I swear, if you hide anything from us, a whole family could be destroyed just like Audrey; I am sure you wouldn't want that Carlos," Edelbert shouted.

Carlos became nervous, he moved away from Edelbert as if to shelter himself from a blow coming his way, "I swear I don't know nothing, you know as much as I do," he screeched while defending his face with his elbow.

"I was born in this town, and people talk; rumours have always had it that Bramwells is haunted, just like the Abbey ruins. I have always kept Audrey away from either till the thomsons moved in, they were very nice that we could not ignore them, because of that, whatever spirit that lies here, Audrey got attacked, and that is why she is dead, because we were nice to them," Carlos expressed.

His eyes were steaming with tears, "My dear Audrey! She is gone forever because of them!" he sobbed and sobbed. Edelbert felt sorry for him and embrassed him, in the effort of comforting him. "It is not your fault, nor Audrey's that this is happening, you have got to look out for each other, right Carlos!" Edelbert stated.

In the mean time, Father Francis was recovering from his ordeal, he was sipping the water that I had brought to him.

"A sip of water will cool me down, because I was in the furnacel," he whispered.

"I got swallowed down by your bathroom, and ended up at the Abbey. From there I had to figure out which way was going to lead me back to your cottage. Father Santos still lives, and together with vicar Simms! I saw them at the Abbey; it was the silver coins that saved me from being swallowed forever in the eternal furnace. I saw Audrey as well, she has become one of them," he uttered.

Carlos and Edelbert were walking in, as Father Francis was finishing uttering his sentence. "Audrey in eternal furnace!" Carlos shouted, "I will not let that happen! You caused this Thomson! Audrey and I should never have got involved with your shenanigan" he shouted.

He tried lushing out at dad, but Edelbert stopped him. "Calm down Carlos, I am sure there is a way of stopping all this," Edelbert said calmly.

Carlos started sobbing some more, "My dear Audrey, gone forever!"

"Somebody give him a drink!" mum shouted.

So Sophia went to the kitchen and got him some brandy. "I will take it straight," Carlos insisted.

He galloped it down in seconds, as if he were a man quenching his thirst. Within a few minutes he went quiete, the alcohol had got to him so fast, Sophia then took him upstairs to the guest bedroom where he slept soundly.

"Now we can talk!" mum said proudly, as if she ridding off some insane person trying to thwart her progressions; but of cause we all knew Carlos was not insane, a bit neurotic yes, but insane, no!

As Carlos slept soundly, we all tried to figure out what might have gone wrong with the exorcism. Mum decided to make some breakfast for Father Francis first.

"You will think better with a full stomach," she said.

He felt more obliged, so he accepted the offer. While mum was cooking, the rest of us were brainstorming.

"Something went wrong when we did the exorcism, but I can't think what it is," said Father Francis.

Edelbert paced up and down, then said,

"You don't think it is Carlos? Do you? the guy seems to be hiding something; perhaps he subottaged the whole thing. Maybe he is protecting something."

Mum could hear from the kitchen, she shouted, "Carlos!, you must be joking, the guy is like an embisal, he does whatever we tell him to do; Him! Oh no!"

# CHAPTER 16

Time passed, Father Francis had had his breakfast, and we were still brainstorming.
"I will have to leave you soon, the parish needs me," he said soon after finishing his breakfast. "But I will be back mid week, in the mean time if anything drastic happens, you know how to reach me."

"But it's not over yet," said mum. "You can't leave us in limbo like this."

"Yeh! you can't do that," we all begged.

"Don't you have anybody to take over your sermons while you help us," asked dad.

"I know it's not easy, but unfortunately no, I have got to go. I will be in touch," replied father Francis.

After he finished his breakfast, he gathered his stuff, and left.

"So what now?" cried Edelbert.

"We need father Francis! I guess in the mean time, we carry on as usual till something happens, then we can call him back," dad responded.

"He said he will be back mid week, so why don't we just wait till then," said Sophia.

"I guess, tommorrow is Monday, it will be work as usual, Carlos will return home tonight, Suzanna and Charlotte will stay with him till father Francis' return. Sophia, mum, and I will be fine here, and Edelbert is back at work tomorrow! so that solves it," dad said.

Somehow, I wasn't convinced. Deep inside I felt this was just the beginning of something really dark. I thought to myself, 'why would father Francis bail out so quick, it was beyond him.'

As daylight grew, mum and dad decided to retreat to bed, Edelbert and Charlotte left for his flat, so I was left all alone with Sophia. Sophia decided to go to bed, she was so exhausted by it all. I was left all alone, just waiting for Carlos to get up, so that I could take him back to his cottage. Carlos was sleeping soundly.

I got fed up with waiting and decided to go to bed myself. I fixed myself a hot water bottle, some cocoa, and before long I was in La-la land. I slept like a baby, and if I may say so, so did mum and dad. We were only woken up by Carlos' voice when he stared, he was shouting Audrey's name. Mum and dad woke up, that is when they decided that it was time for Carlos to return to his cottage. Since Charlotte was out with Edelbert, I had to go alone with Carlos to his cottage. He didn't put up a fight, he was as gentle as puppy dog,

"You will stay with me right Suzanna!" he bellowed as mum and dad led him to the door.

"Of cause I will," I responded.

I led him through the narrow little lane back to his cottage, "I miss Audrey!" he kept saying.

"I feel it is all my fault that she is gone!" he lamented.

"I need to tell you something!" he said.

I was tired and felt all alone, I didn't care anymore. "Ithink a little rest will do you some good," I said as we got inside his cottage.

"Yeh! I guess you are right, but I want to confess! I feel it is all my fault!" Carlos exclaimed. "I owe you and your family an explanation," he replied.

I wasn't interested to hear anything coming from his mouth, I was tired.

"It's not your fault Carlos, why don't you get some rest!" I yelled.

So Carlos timidly went upstairs to his bedroom where he remained for a good four hours.

I sat in the library feeling bored, then I decided to look at different books, I couldn't find anything interesting; that is when Charlotte burst in unexpectedly.

"How come you are back so early?" I asked.

"Edelbert has gone to work, he has got a lot of paper work to catch up with, besides mum and dad directly send me here," she replied.

"Aren't I glad to see you, it has been so boring here without you, Carlos is upstairs, possibly asleep," I said.

"Everything has gone so wrong, what do you think is going to happen next? I hope Edelbert is alright, we dragged him in to all this. I believe father Francis is our only hope," she said.

"The ritual didn't go well, some things were not meant to happen, for instance what happened to Audrey, and afterwards what happened to father Francis. Carlos behaved rather weirdly, he acted like he was hiding something. He is probably not as vulnerable as he puts out to be. Peharps we were meant to do the rirual here as well, remember historically the two cottages are linked with the Abbey. This is the place where the monks lived, and Bramwells is where father Carlos lived. What if Carlos happens to be a direct descendant of father Carlos, and had changed his second name. Well I am just assuming, "I added.

Charlotte was ramaging through Carlos' books, she lifted her head up, appearing lost in thought, then she said, "But Carlos' second name is not Carlos, it happens to be a coincidence that his first name is Carlos. It could be Audrey who could be the descedent?. Listen! she said to me, there is no point speculating, we need facts, evidence, and a solution to this problem."

"We should dig from Carlos when he comes downstairs," I suggested. "Sounds like a plan," Charlotte grinned away.

We spend the rest of the afternoon ramaging through the library, hoping to find something, a book, newspaper article, or anything that could be related to the happenings, but without success. After a while Carlos came downstairs, he was a lot a calmer, besides not having any time to grieve over Audrey. We had to do something, all of us, to help him grieve and come to terms with what was going on. The night before had been long, tiring and scary at the same time, that is why we did not discuss Audrey at all. However, when Carlos came downstairs, it was the perfect time to talk to him about Audrey, and console him. Charlotte made some tea, Carlos was sobbing away. We decided to take Carlos with us to Bramwells, and have lunch with him; mum and dad were there, and Sophia was working. We knew that mum and dad would be better at dealing with Carlos, and grieving over Audrey.

We got home, mum and dad were up, both of them on the edge; Charlotte and I dragged them to the kitchen while Carlos sat comfortably in the lounge. We discussed Audrey, and how we were going to help Carlos deal with his loss. As we surfaced from the kitchen to the lounge, Carlos was sobbing away.

"We are all grieving over Audrey," dad began, "it is truelly tragic, none of us wanted this to happen, but we are going to do our own memorial service of Audrey, but I feel for now, it should just be us, and father Francis. I don't think we should trust anyone, till all this is sorted," he sobbed. Mum was crying as well, which made me and Charlotte sob as well. Mum and dad embrassed Carlos as they sobbed away, and Carlos was as reciprocative.

"I want to confess! it is all my fault, I beg for your forgiveness!" Carlos yelled.

Mum and dad held him tighter, they could feel his pains.

"You have got nothing to confess Carlos! it is all our fault," mum said. "The problems started here, remember Carlos; and we dragged you and Audrey into all this. So it is us who should apologise," mum sobbed.

"You don't get it! it is my fault! can you forgive me," he insisted.

Dad held Carlos' hand reassuaring,

"You don't know what you are saying because you are grieving! We will do a funeral ceremony for Audrey, when father Francis return, it will be private of course," he said.

"If you say so, Ed, but I know I have done some very bad things!" Carlos replied.

It was Monday of cause, but father Francis was to return on the Wednesday, and we were going to find out more then. The day went by, and before long, Sophia finished work and was back home home; a few hours later Edelbert finished work, he came straight to Bramwells. Edelbert came to Bramwells and persuaded Charlotte and I to go with him; we were headed for the local library. "I want to show you something!" he said.

As it worked out Edelbert, during his lunch break from hospital, had gone to the library to dig more about Bramwells' history. By then it was about 5.30pm, the libraries were to close at 6.30pm, Sophia was back from work; so Sophia, Charlotte and I, went with Aldelbert to the library, we left mum and dad consoling Carlos. We got to the library, Aldebert had this book which he had laid aside. It was about spells, human sacrifice and the after life. In the book lay secrets about Bramwell cottage and the famous Abbey. It explained everything about the brotherhood that existed during the time of father Santos, and how to exorcise the spiirit that had plagued many from during its conception to present day. It spoke of father Santos, Bramwells, and Carlos' cottage; human sacrifices and the perpetualness of the cult. Edelbert particularly emphasized on the power of control and manipulation. He read a chapter in front of us, about how the spirit works through sensing human weakness. So Audrey died because she lacked human will power to survive. These spirits work on your weakness, if you appear weak, they will get the best of you; but if you fight, it will be harder for these spirits to defeat you." Edelbert read.

"So whatever it is? it is a test of our stamina?" Charlotte replied.

"Yes! that is the idea, so whatever it is, do not surrender to it, because if you do, that is you done and dusted," he replied.

The book also says that, if the exorcism fails, it means that you don't have the right books, if one book is fake, the exorcism will fail," Edelbert read.

Charlotte and I pondered why the exorcism failed; maybe one of the books was fake. Father Francis brought the right book, so maybe the book we got from Audrey's was fake; a replica? So maybe either Carlos or Audrey hid the real book, and replaced it with a fake. I thought Carlos was hiding something from us. If he did, then peharps he did not deserve any sympanthy from us. Edelbert breathed heavily, then continued,

"There is something else, early this morning while driving to work, some man was following me. He was driving a black pick up truck, with tinted windows. He followed me, bumper to pumber right behind me, and only drove off when I got to the hospital. And when I left the hospital, I saw the same car just outside the hospital gates. This time his passenger window was wound down."

"What are you talking about?" Charlotte interrupted. "I saw him, he appeared to be in his sixties, grey beard and he was wearing a red clock with the hood covering his head. It was like a clock that we saw father Santos wearing at the Abbey. He stared at me, then when I drove into your drive, he drove off. It felt like he was threatening me."

I shook my head then responded,

"It feels like there is many of them involved, we better tell dad, because this is getting more and more dangerous. He might ring the police, but then again, there could be some of them, working there. It's like you can't trust anyone." "What are we going to do?" asked Edelbert. Edelbert started scratching his yarn of blonde hair.

"Stop doing that, otherwise you will go bald!" shouted Charlotte. He fidgeted with his hair some more, then sat down, croutched over with his head in between his legs.

"I am way out of my line, I don't know what to do? Tell me what to do Charlotte, and I will do it," he said reaching out for Charlotte's hand. Charlotte put her other arm around him then said, "It will be alright, everything will be fine."

I left the drawing room, then went to the lounge to speak to dad about what Edelbert had told me and Charlotte. "Why aren't I surprised," dad responded after hearing of Edelbert's story. "This place is full of it, isn't it. Anything goes around here, imagined or unimagined. You can't dispute that! that's for sure.

# CHAPTER 17

After the exorcism at the Abbey, none of us ever spoke of vicar Simms again. As far as the villagers were concerned, vicar Simms was a missing person, and they were still searching for him.

We heard knocking on the door, dad rushed to the door, he was hoping that it could be father Francis.

'I am the new vicar of the parish,' the voice went.

We all rushed to the door, to meet the new vicar. In came this short, rather plump little man with twinkling little green eyes. He was bold, with very little hairs either side of his rather large head, grey beard, and a protruding forehead. He wore black trousers, black jacket, and a white shirt with a priest's dog collar. He stepped into the cottage quickly, without being invited in.

"I am vicar Dowling, and I will be taking over from vicar Simms," he smiled softly.

"Won't you come in," dad said. It was a little bit too late to invite him in as he had walked in already.

"That is rather odd," I whispered to Charlotte. "He walks in without being invited."

Dad took him to the lounge, and we all joined them.

He was excited to meet the family.

"I heard you were pretty close to vicar Simms," he asked. Dad took a huge sigh, cleared his throat, then replied, "Yes! somewhat. We haven't been in this town that long,

so we knew very little of him, even though he visited us quiete regularly. His disappearance is very sad for all of us. Do you happen to have any leads on what might have happened to him vicar," dad asked conscientiously.

"Yeh! that's right vicar, we are all worried about him," bursted mum. I nudged Charlotte's arm, and who in turn nudged Sophia who was sat right next to her. Sophia then nudged Dr Edelbert who by then was looking perplexed.

"Well, rumours have it that, he got himself mixed up with some cult, that he either vanished with the cult, or the members killed him and hid his body," the vicar replied. He looked at all of us suspiciously.

"You don't happen to know anything about this, do you?" he asked venomously. By then he was standing by the fire place, with his feet astride, and his arms stretched resting on either ends of the fire place, with a dominating pause. We felt quiete intimidated, here was a complete stranger in our house and behaving precariously.

"We don't know anything vicar," dad replied. "I guess that's alright then," he replied.

Dad appeared uneasy, and so did we all.

"My last parish was in a small town called Stantley, a few miles from here," he said.

None of us had heard of the place before, not even Carlos who had geographical knowledge of our town and it's humble surroundings.

"I seem to recognise you from somewhere," he said to Carlos.

"Peharps it's my imagination running wild." Carlos seemed nervous.

He replied, "Trust me sir, I have never seen you before in my life."

He started hyperventilating, "Jane and Ed please excuse me, I have got to go home," he said frantically.

"I wouldn't mind if Dr Edelbert comes with me," he added.

"Very well," Edelbert replied.

Carlos started huffing and puffing as he gathered his stuff, and reaching for the front door, Edelbert was right behind him.

"I won't be long," Edelbert shouted as he banged the front door behind him.

Charlotte and I were bemused by the whole thing. "Don't you think you should go with them?" I whispered to Charlotte.

"Of cause," she replied.

Charlotte excused herself from the unpopular vicar, to join Carlos and Edelbert. Outside the weather had changed, it was a nice shiny day by forecast, but then in a period of minutes, it had turned icy cold. The clouds had turned grey, the grass in the front garden of Carlos' home had frost that even the front gate had frosted over. His whole front garden was pecked with hundreds black crows. Carlos and Dr Edelbert had seen them but had chosen to ignore them. Charlotte caught up with them struggling to release the lever of the gate because it was frozen tightly. Edelbert tried with all his might to force the gate open, and eventually he succeeded.

"Here we are," he exclaimed as he led the way out of Bramwells.

"How can weather change so drastically? I mean in a matter of seconds from being hot to extremely cold," said Charlotte.

"I don't know," replied Edelbert.

Edelbert led the way till they got to Carlos'.

In the meantime back at Bramwells, I was becoming fed up of vicar Dowlings' presence, he kept asking questions about vicar Simms, what we thought of him, and when we last saw him. He was a curiosity, dad thought to himself. He figured he could dig a little from him about the cult.

"What have you heard about this cult," he asked. Vicar Dowlings paused a little then replied,

"All sorts really. I must say there is some bad elements in this town, but I haven't exactly come across them yet," he added.

"That Carlos seems to be hiding something, perhaps he knows more than he acts out to be. I suggest search in his cottage, and there you will find the key," he continued. "Carlos is a very close member of the family, we look out for him and his wife Audrey. For you to talk like that about him, I take it as an offence. I bet you didn't know he has got a wife?" dad asked.

Vicar Dowlings laughed sacarstically,

"I know he has got a wife. The problem is, people in the parish are concerned about her because they haven't seen her for a while. Maybe her disappearance is linked with vicar Simms weird disappearance, and it's the cult of cause."

"I think you should leave," dad said scornfully. Vicar Dowlings took a big sigh, then replied

"I was about to anyway, I had just thought I should drop by and introduce myself."

Dad led him to the front door, he couldn't wait to get rid of him.

"Let me know if you find anything at Carlos'," he shouted on his way out.

Dad was angry, he banged the front door, then muttered, "good riddance."

I decided to go to Carlos' because I was curious of what might be happening there. I grabbed my coat then ran outside without telling mum and dad where I was going. The whole garden was frozen, and the cold was killing, entering my bones like an ice splinter. I couldn't explain that, it wasn't even winter. Mum's roses were just breaking off the stems and so was the leaves of the garden trees, with the help of a gush wind that swept through Bramwells. I struggled hard to open the gate as the hinges were all frozen, then stepping out of Bramwells I realised that everywhere else the weather was nice and shiny. I caught a glimpse of vicar Dowlings, he had parked his pick up truck behind some bush outside the corner of Bramwells. It was well hidden there, a black truck with tinted windows.

Why did he park there, somewhere hidden, especially with us having a big driveway and parking space at Bramwells. I stood there for a while spying on him, he took out a little book from his pocket, and started scribbling something on it, then got in his van and drove off.

I got to Carlos', his garden was covered in frost as well, then I knew that dark force was active again. Fear crippled me as I knocked on Carlos' door and Edelbert came to answer the door.

"Isn't it strange that only these two houses are covered in frost and nowhere else. You don't think what I think it is do you, "he said anxiously.

"Unfortunately so," I replied as I got inside Carlos' cottage.

Inside Carlos' cottage, it was freezing cold, Charlotte and Carlos where sat by the fire, both of them rubbing their hands from the cold.

"We can't seem to be warming up at all," said Carlos while quivering away.

"Do you think it's happening again Suzanna?" Charlotte asked.

"Afraid so," I replied. "I think that new vicar Dowling is part of it. I saw him, soon after you left, he had parked his pick up truck hidden behind the bushes just outside Bramwells. He then took out a little book from his pocket and scribbled something before driving off. That appeared kind of suspicious, and besides we all heard him talk, he was insinuating something. It was kind of intimidating for all of us."

Edelbert started pacing up and down, and rubbing his yarn of hair, a regular habit of his when confronted with a stressful situation.

"Did you say a pick up truck?" he questioned.

"What colour was it? did it have tinted windows?" he questioned some more.

"Why do you ask? I replied.

"It was black in colour and yes it had tinted windows." "Yeh! that is the same truck that followed me this morning on my way to work, and was outside the hospital gate," Edelbert responded.

"It's has got to be him then," we all replied. "He is part of it then," said Charlotte.

As soon as Charlotte finished her sentence, a gush of wind swept through the fireplace, putting out the fire. Frost appeared in the house, working it's way from the front door, leaving us extremely cold. Charlotte and I ran upstairs to collect some blankets. We covered Carlos with most of the blankets as he was the most vulnerable out of all of us, but that didn't help. Frost started working it's way on Carlos, his fingers got covered in it. And this was the time to escape, we headed for the door, and we were going to go back to Bramwells. Edelbert tried opening the front door, but it was completely frozen. Carlos by then, frost was working it's way on to his face, he was struggling for breathe. Charlotte ran to the basement to see if she could find a hammer or crow bar so we could try to open the door. She came back with a hammer. Edelbert tried and tried to break the front door open, but to no success.

"Try the basement window," Carlos said as he struggled for breathe.

In a hurried state, we raced for the basement, Charlotte and I were supporting Carlos shoulder to shoulder. We got in the basement, of which was frozen as well, the whole house was frozen. Edelbert was holding the hammer, he smushed the little window, which was just about big enough for all of us to climb out. The first person out was Charlotte, then Carlos, then me. Just before Edelbert tried climbing out, tonnes of snow appeared from nowhere covering the window from outside.

"Help! help! I am stuck in here!" Edelbert cried.

He couldn't clear the snow himself as it came from the outside. His fingers were frosting and so was his face, till he couldn't talk no more. While stuck in there, temperature started changing in the house, it became extremely hot, all the frost melted away till Edelbert was sweating, his body was turning red from the heat. His speech returned.

"Help! I am burning!" he screamed. Charlotte and I hurried in clearing the snow blocking the window, and we eventually managed to drag him out. The snow managed to cool him down while Carlos was still freezing away. Charlotte helped Edelbert, and I helped Carlos till we got out of Carlos' yard and headed for Bramwells.

We got to Bramwells and the gate was still frozen, the garden was covered in snow about thirty inches high. Charlotte and I battled with the gate, and eventually managed to open it. By the time we got to front door Carlos was barely able to stand. Mum opened the door in awe, firstly seeing the state that Carlos and Elbert was in, and secondly the state of the garden and all that snow.

"Ed!" she called dad. Dad was resting in bed trying to recover from all the escapedes.

"We have got problems! come quick! and the garden is covered in snow, and it's not even winter yet!" she yelled.

Dad came running down the stairs, he was in his pyjamas. He ran down fast that he nearly slipped on the stairs. Mum led Carlos by the fire where he started warming up, she then went to the kitchen to make him a hot cup of cocoa. Carlos and Elbert remained speechless as Charlotte and I told mum and dad what had just happened.

"What are we to do?" said dad. "I guess the best we can do is to stay close together, and look out for each other.

"Why don't you ring father Francis, he said that we can call him if things get worse," said mum.

"That's the only thing to do dad," cried Charlotte. Sophia remained in awe, and was speechless just like Carlos and Edelbert.

"I will ring him later, let the dust settle first," replied dad. Carlos finished his cocoa and his colour was returning after warming up by the fire. Mum, dad, Charlotte and I carried on talking about what had just happened and I told them about vicar Dowling, how he had parked his truck hidden behind a bush just outside Bramwells. I told them that he was likely to be the person who had followed Edelbert on his way to the hospital, and watched Edelbert by the hospital after he finished work.

Dad decided to go outside in the garden to see the damage caused by the ice, and also to see whether he could find some of clue to what might be going on. He stepped outside in his slippers and winter coat, to his horror the garden was filled with black crows. On one end of the garden was a fleet of the black crows, and on the other was a colony of black cats. He walked further down the garden towards the gate, peered all around outside the gate, and there he spotted vicar Dowlings black truck. In the truck was a man wearing a red hood, just the red hood he had seen father Carlos wearing. He couldn't see the face of the man, so he decided to walk further torwards the truck. As he got closer and closer, the man drove off, and so he couldn't tell for sure if it was vicar Dowling. Walking back from the gate, he tried shooshing the cats and birds away. The birds attacked dad, pecking him on the face and hands mainly. He ran torwards the front door, and managed to get in the cottage and shut the door behind them. They were screeching and screeching right by the front door and not going away. The noise was more or less defeaning, that we all covered our ears with our hands. Mum ran to dad's aid, she got some antiseptic liquid to clean his wounds.

"What was that about!" dad yelled. He was gasping for breathe.

"Those things could have easily killed me, imagine if the door was locked what could have happened.

That's it!" yelled dad. I am calling father Francis."

Without wasting time, he picked the phone up and called father father Francis. There was no answer, the phone kept ringing and ringing, and still he didn't pick up.

"I will try again later," said dad. "There is no other way of stopping this except through him," he added.

Carlos became restless, he began to fret. He got up and started pacing up and down, his face looked vacant.

"I want to go home! I want to go home! let me go home!" he shouted.

Edelbert tried calming him down. He put his hand on his shoulder and tried leading him back to his seat by the fire. Carlos pushed him away, and was heading torwards the door.

"You don't want to go out there Carlos! not with those things out there, they will peck you to death!" shouted dad.

He grabbed Carlos hand, and tried forcing him away from the door. He pushed dad to the ground.

"Let me go! let me go!" he persisted.

He battled with dad and Edelbert, till eventually dad punched him on the head, and he passed out. Dad and Edelbert dragged him upstairs to one of the spare rooms, where he laid asleep, and undisturbed.

A moments peace as so much desired was becoming impossible, despite Carlos passing out. The birds carried on screeching by the front door and now the black cats gathered and sat by the front window ledge mewing. They were scratching the front window as if trying to get inside. The sight was frightening, and I guess that is what led Carlos over the edge. Dad tried once more to ring father Francis, but still there was still no reply.

"How come he ain't picking up," dad said.

By then the sun was setting, outside it was beginning to darken, the sky turning grey, but those black crows were still screeching outside the front door, and the black cats petched by the window seel mewing and scratching the window.

Dr Edelbert's padger went off, he was on call, and had to leave to go to the hospital.

"I don't have to go, I can give an excuse, like I'm sick or something," he murmmered.

"What the hell, you go," uttered dad. "I'm sure we will manage. I will drive you there, and I will pick you. Get your things now, and I will drop you," dad insisted.

Edelbert looked at Charlotte, then asked, "Should I go?" Without hesitation, Charlotte replied, "Yes."

It was enough for Edelbert, he got his bag and he was ready to go.

"I'm ready!" he said to dad. By then dad had read his mind and was on his way to fetch the car keys.

"We are going in my car! and I will pick you up in my car!" he insisted.

Without question Edelbert agreed, he kissed Charlotte and promised a prompt return. Dad got his keys, and Edelbert was right behind him, he was dreading opening the front door to all them birds and cats.

"Follow me behind!" he said to Edelbert.

Edelbert was right behind him, he looked at Charlotte, then winked at her, and whispered,

"Wish me luck."

Dad opened the front door, the peck of birds were waiting, they started pecking on him, and then Edelbert, till they made their way to the car. They kept flipping them, and kicking the flipping black cats away. They both made it to the car unharmed. Dad drove away, the snow still riddled the grounds of Bramwells. When approaching the hospital, dad and Edelbert spotted the black pick up truck again, it seemed vicar Dowling was following them again.

"Once I am inside the hospital, he can't follow me there, I will be safe," said Edelbert.

"Ring me otherwise," dad insisted. "Don't be foolish enough to go your own way, they will attack you easier that way," insisted dad.

# CHAPTER 18

Dad dropped off Edelbert at the front of Saint Marys hospital, utterly ignoring vicar Dowlings presence and threat.

"They feed on your fears! they feed on your fears!" dad kept repeating to himself.

"Do not surrender to their intimidations, that is how their satanic cult feeds, from your fears," he repeated.

He rubbed his his chin as he would naturally do when nervous. He started reciting a verse from the bible, Psalms 28, "though I walk through the shadow of death, I shall fear no evil"

Miraculously it seemed to strengthen him, that he drove past vicar Dowlings without feeling any fear what so ever. He drove back home feeling that his faith could save us all. When we heard his car drive back, we were surprised to look outside and saw that the black cats were gone and so was the black crows. Carlos was up and was as calm as ever. "Where is Edelbert?" he asked. He had developed a natural liking to him, and Carlos had always felt safer with Edelbert was around.

"I don't hear the crows! and all them cats gone!" Carlos said.

"Yeh Carlos they are gone, call it a leap of faith hey," dad replied.

"What is that poor boy getting himself into. If I was him, I would run a mile from this place," said Carlos.

"He had to go to work, I drove him there," replied dad. "We have to keep on behaving as normal as we can. We can't allow this entity to run our lives, nor accept living in fear. I think it feeds on our fears as father Francis said. "You are right Ed," responded Carlos. "We have to carry on with our lives."

"Speaking of which, I have got to try ringing him again," said dad. "If I don't get a reply, it means I have to drive there. Who will go with me? any volunteers?" asked dad.

Charlotte and I volunteered, Sophia and mum would stay with Carlos.

"That settles it then, we would be back in time to pick Edelbert up from hospital. Anyhow let me try ringing him now," he insisted.

Dad picked the phone up and rung father Francis. This time he was very patient on the phone, the phone rang and rang and still there was no reply. He put the phone down and decided not to go to father Francis' until early next morning as it was getting dark. Edelbert rang from the hospital, he was going to spend the night at the hospital.

That evening mum was passive, unlike her usual over the top personality. She made dinner quietely in the kitchen, she never asked for help. Her level of concentration was shocking, she made the best dinner ever. It was shoulder of lamb, new potatoes minted and rosted asparugus, accompanied by a sweet mint sauce.

"Dinner is ready," she called in a subdued manner.

The table was set very neatly, with her napkins temporarily imprisoned by the golden rings that were only meant to be used on christmas day.

"What is the occassion? why all this extra effort," said dad.

"Why don't you all sit down and enjoy. I will not allow this entity to overtake our lives, so today we are going to eat well," replied mum.

She started sobbing, as each one of us pulled our chairs round the dinner table. Carlos' mood was good and excitable. "That looks really good Jane, I can't wait to tuck in, I am vamished. It is a pity Edelbert ain't here to enjoy the feast with us," Carlos exclaimed.

He sat down and tucked into his dinner. the expression on his face as he took each mouthful was extra ordinary. His face shone with joy as he munched into his dinner.

"I take it we have got a nice pudding Jane." Carlos grinned.

"Audrey used to make nice dinners for me, and rosted lamb was one of my favourites," he added.

"We have got stewed apples and custard for our pudding Carlos," mum replied.

"Audrey used to make that too," responded Carlos excitedly.

We all enjoyed our meal except mum. She had worked so hard to put such a spread, and yet she hardly ate herself. Throughout the meal she kept getting up and looking out the window.

"I hope Edelbert is alright," she kept saying.

She was kind of hoping he was going to show up anytime.

"Stop worrying about him, Charlotte isn't. He is spending the night at the hospital, and he is going to be alright," urged dad.

"I'm not worrying, I just wished he was here to share with us this special meal," replied mum.

"Nothing is going to happen to him mum," urged Charlotte. "See, them horrible birds and cats are gone."

I looked at Charlotte, then said, "We should all enjoy this hour before something else happens."

"You are right Suzanna," grinned Carlos as he wiped clean the last bit of dinner off his plate.

"I'm ready for my afters Jane," Carlos said excitedly.

"I could have easily licked that plate Jane, it was delicious," added Carlos.

By then we all had finished eating our dinner, mum collected the plates and started dishing the stewed apples and custard.

"Do you need a hand mum?" asked Sophia.

Mum carried on dishing out the pudding, her mind was so far away that she didn't hear her.

"Mum! do you need a hand!" shouted Sophia.

This time she heard her, she shook her head then replied, "No I'm fine."

Her mind was so far away hence her behaviour like a burning matyer who suffers silently.

We had our afters and thoroughly enjoyed, except her of cause, Carlos cleared his plate like before quiete happily. After, we all retired to the living room, dad tried ringing father Francis again, but to his dismay there was no reply again. Mum got her cross stitching out, she did a little bit, got fed up, and started putting the left overs from dinner in a plastic bag, ready to feed her chickens.

"Are you alright in there?" dad shouted at mum.

By then he was busy reading his newspaper in the drawing room.

"I'm fine, soon I will go tend to my chickens," she replied. She started ruttling the dishes in a nervous stupor that the noise was herrondeous, almost deafening.

"Will you stop that!" dad shouted. "I will feed the chickens myself," he insisted.

She carried on rattling the dishes, then replied crossly, "I am fine, I don't need your help."

Dad responded by banging the lounge door shut, that we don't need hear the rattling.

She then responded by bursting into the lounge holding a big sharp knife, waving it at dad. She screamed,

"You are part of this aren't you Ed! you are responsible for putting this family through all this! I never wanted to move here in the first place, it was your stupid idea. A fresh start hey! look where it has led us. I will never forgive you for this!" she yelled, then banged the door behind her.

Dad did not react for a while, he carried on reading his paper. She carried on rattling the dishes, only then did dad react. He got off the coutch violently then shouted,

"Your mum is a stupid woman! She wanted the move more than any one of us did. She hated the city, and hated everybody else who lived in it. I did it for her," he persisted. He walked out to the kitchen, picked up the bag of left overs and chicken feed, and went out to feed the chickens. He was out in the garden for a good hour, pacing up and down. When he came back in Carlos was in bed, and so was mum. Mum had gone to bed sulcking, she had left the kitchen light on, and the tap running. It was Charlotte who realised it and had turned both off. It seemed dad had become cross with everyone, talking and answering back sharply in a dismissive manner. He was fed up and decided to go to bed as well. He didn't speak of what we were going to do the following morning, no mention of Edelbert nor father Francis.

After he was gone to bed, Sophia and I accompanied Charlotte outside in the garden to have a cigarrette. We spoke of what we going to do the following morning. We spoke of Edelbert, father Francis, and Carlos. Charlotte and I were still suspicious of Carlos, we both felt he was hiding something from us. Eventually we grew tired of the speculations, and retired to bed.

# CHAPTER 19

Early next morning Edelbert rang. He was ready to be picked up, so dad went to pick him up from the hospital. Nothing unusual had happened at the hospital. They got back to Bramwells, by then, Charlotte, Sophia and I were up while mum and Carlos were still in bed. We were ready to go with dad to father Francis'. Edelbert was going to stay at Bramwells with mum, Carlos, and Charlotte. I must say, I was a bit disappointed with the agreement because Charlotte and I had always ventured together, but here now, Edelbert needed her as well.

Dad was ready to go and so was Sophia and I. Before long we were on the main road heading to father Francis' parish in Sutland. Back at Bramwells Charlotte and Edelbert decided to go out for a coffee in the village. They left mum and Carlos fast asleep, each one of them trying to escape through sleep. Charlotte and Edelbert knew that, so they were going to be out for most of the morning and possibly afternoon.

In the village they bumped into old Ted who wasn't so delighted to meet them. In fact old Ted had tried hiding from them when they saw him at the market. He hid behind some clothes at some market stall. It was too late as Charlotte had spotted him already.

"Good morning Ted!" shouted Charlotte from right behind him.

He jumped with fright, then replied,

"So it is you, Charlotte Thomson. How is your father? and how is everything at Bramwells?" he questioned.

"Everyone is fine Ted," replied Charlotte.

She introduced Edelbert to him, and before long they got acquainted. Edelbert took an immediate liking to old Ted as he enjoyed talking a lot about the history of our town. He knew everybody, and he knew everything. There was no secrets that could be hidden he did not know of, and of cause Edelbert liked that about him. Ted got talking, that was good, despite the fact that he had tried hiding from them.

'The fish took the bate,' as Charlotte later put it.

"You know the tale of Bramwells, and that it is all true. I bet you have been experiencing some things there, from when you moved in," said old Ted.

He scratched his nose then proceeded,

"They believe that the old couple who live next door to you have always been involved, especially the old man Carlos. They have lived there for decades, and they believe her family have always lived there, from her parents, and her parents parents. If I were you and your family, I wouldn't trust either of them. Their children got to learn about their involvement, and they grew detached from them, that is why they don't visit anymore."

Old Ted was an old man, grey haired, short in stature and rather stout. He spoke with a lisp, that a few villagers used to tease him saying that his parents dropped him when he was a baby and that is why he spoke like that. He didn't take much notice of it though, and just carried on with his humble life. He was married, had a couple of kids and a couple of grand kids who were grown and working in the village. Like Carlos and Audrey, he was born in the village and never left. Old Mrs Shivers was his wife, and knew Audrey very well. They had often spent a lot of time together doing some of charity work or the other. We all knew Mrs Shivers, her generosity and talkative nature. Mum had met her a few times at the womens union and did love her kind nature.

"Not many families have survived living in that cottage. They all seem to die from some fire accident. It is my understanding that if you try to leave, you will end up endangering yourselves even more. So stay there, and try and fight this thing. I wish you well, and

I guess it is only your faith that can save you now," said Ted. He then winked at us.

"Do you know anybody who could help us?" asked Edelbert.

"No I don't," replied Ted.

He scratched his nose again, then added,

"The whole village is part of it. If I was you, I wouldn't trust anyone."

"We are doomed then," Charlotte responded. "Have you met the new vicar yet, vicar Dowling? "We have," replied Charlotte.

"Oh my! I feel sorry for you.

Still, I would like to stand here and chat but I have to go before I get into any trouble. Good day to you, and good luck," old Ted said then he walked away and disappeared in the crowd.

In the mean time, Sophia, dad, and I were approaching father Francis town; the town was deserted, not a single person was about. It was kind of bizarre for us, empty streets without a flicker of sound. We got to father Francis' vicarage, it was silent, not a figure in sight. Dad knocked at his vicarage, but there was no reply. He knocked and knocked, much to our dispair, nobody answered. Dad grew impatient, till he started knocking violently, and eventually an old woman came to answer the door. She was an old nun dressed in her hermit outfit.

"What can I do for you?" she asked as if in a smearing way. "We want to talk to father Francis," dad replied as he he forcefully pushed himself in the vicarage.

She had no chance to force us away, as dad was already inside the vicarage.

"I guess you are welcome," she smiled sarcastically. "Where is father Francis?" dad prompted.

"He is up here, sick," she replied unshakably.

Dad forced himself upstairs, followed by me, Charllotte, and the old nun of cause. When we got upstairs, dad had to go through a few doors first, till eventually, he found the room where father Francis lay in bed sick and helpless. To our dismay, his whole body was covered in boils, and popping out of these boils was big slugs. We had seen those slugs before from Audrey.

"Oh my God!" dad exclaimed. "They have got to him as well, just like to Audrey! We have to help him!" he shouted. The whole bed was covered with slimmy slugs, slithering everywhere in the bedding. He couldn't move, but lay there motionless like a drunken man drowning in his own urine.

"Can he talk?" dad asked anxiously looking at me and Sophia. The old nun remained downstairs, and we all wondered why she didn't follow us upstairs.

"Father Francis! father Francis! can you hear me!" shouted dad.

He shook him by the shoulder, but there was no response.

"We need you father Francis, you can't let us down now!" mourned dad.

Still there was no response. He appeared comatosed. "Shouldn't you take him to the hospital?" I asked the old nun.

The old nun paced up and down the little room that father Francis lay in. She reached out to his bed and held his hand firmly, then replied,

"It is his wish that if he is going to die, he would rather die here than in a hospital. It is our policy that we respect each others' wishes even up to death."

She then wrapped some rosary beads around his wrist. "I shall leave you with him for a little while, then when you are ready to leave, just let me know, I will be in the foyre," she said gracefully as she reached for the door. "Sister hang on a minute!" shouted dad." You must know something about what is happening to father Francis. Did he ever mention anything to you about Bramwell's cottage?"

The old nun seemed perplexed, she gasped, then replied, "Of cause he did, this is where all these problems are deriving from. He made me swear never to speak of it, and as for calling the doctor, he never wanted that neither," she said in a prudish manner, then walked out of the room, gently closing the door behind her, as you would expect from a modest nun.

Dad was disturbed, but weren't we all, he knelt down and started praying. I had never seen him pray before. He held father Francis' hand, took the rosary beads off father Francis' hand, and then wrapped them round his wrist as he carried on praying. Charlotte and I were humbled, we joined him on the floor and started reciting the Lords prayer with him.

While in the middle of prayer, the humble nun gently opened the door again, then whispered.

"I'm only giving you ten minutes with him, and then you have to leave, because he needs his rest," and then she closed the door again.

After minutes of prayer, father Francis opened his eyes. He grabbed dad by the collar and whispered something in his ear before falling asleep again. Dad sighed, resting his hand on his chin, lost in thought. He got up.

"We have to go," he said. He helped Charlotte and I up, and led us to the door.

"What did he say to you?" Charlotte asked. She was kind of fighting not to leave the room.

"We can't leave him like that, we have got to do something," I expressed.

"We have to go," replied dad. "He wants us to leave."

We walked out of the vicarage without anybody seeing us out. As we drove back home dad remained silent. Neither Charlotte nor I wanted to initiate conversation.

Sophia and Edelbert were still in the village high street. They walked into vicar Dowlings, he was at the market with Carlos assisting him with shopping. Carlos appeared content in his company, chatting away.

"How is life treating you at Bramwells!" shouted Dowlings in a sacarstic manner.

"We are all well, thanks for asking," replied Charlotte.

Edelbert did not say anything, he grabbed Charlotte's and said to her,

"I bet your parents are waiting for us, we better go."

Charlotte smiled at both Carlos and vicar Dowlings before heading on. As they walked through the market they wondered what Carlos was doing with vicar Dowlings.

"There must be a connection between Carlos and Dowlings with what is going on at Bramwells," remarked Edelbert.

"I wonder what that could be? he is probably just being sweet to an old man. Besides we still don't know much about him, so let's not jump into conclusions." said Charlotte.

Charlotte and Edelbert left the village town and headed for home. When they got back to Bramwells; dad, Sophia and I were just pulling in as well in the car park.

"Tell us about your adventure, what did you find out?" Charlotte shouted as she got out of Edelbert's car.

"Not much," I replied from the car, the car window was wound down as we pulled in.

When we were all out of the prospective cars, we chatted for ages in the car port about what we had experienced. Mum was indoors asleep, she got woken up by the chatterings, and so she came outside to join us.

"What about Carlos? do you think he is back from the village town? and is father Dowling still with him?" Sophia asked.

None of us knew, so Sophia, Charlotte, Edelbert and I volunteered to go check on him. When we got to his cottage, father Dowling was just leaving. He greeted us jously, dare I say with a smirk on his face. It was no longer surprising to us anymore because he was always like that with us everytime we crossed paths.

"Be careful with what you are delging into," he said to us as he left Carlos'.

He lifted his bowler hat, then placed it back on his big head again as if to were showing gentlemanly respect, then disappeared behind the wooden gates.

We knocked on Carlos' door, but there was no reply. We knocked over and over again for a good five minutes, but still there was no reply. Charlotte and Edelbert opened the little side gate that led to the back garden and went through and peered through the back windows, but there was no sight of Carlos being in the cottage. Sophia and I peered through the front windows, there was no sight of him, nor any activity in his cottage. They came back to the front to join Sophia and I.

"Maybe Father Dowling killed him," uttered Edelbert. "I doubt it, I think he was told by Father Dowling not to answer the door. The two of them must be hiding something," said Charlotte.

I got worried and decided to call on dad, he would know what to do. I went to Bramwells alone, leaving Sophia, Charlotte and Edelbert. When I got home, dad and I scoured in the garage for some tools that could force open Carlos' door. Dad got a crow bar and a sledge hammer and we went back to Carlos'. Sophia was still banging on the door none stop, and still there was no sign of Carlos. Dad kicked the door several times till it was kind of weak, then he used the sledge hammer till it was open. We dashed into the cottage and spread ourselves everywhere looking for Carlos. He wasn't upstairs, so we went upstairs, spread ourselves again upstairs. Dad found the bathroom to be locked.

"I think he is in the bathroom!" shouted dad. "Carlos! Carlos! are you in there!" dad shouted.

There was no answer. "I am going to kick the door open!" shouted dad again.

He kicked the door. It take much out of him to open the door slightly, the inside chain was hooked so it made it impossible for dad to get in. He got the crow bar and cut the chain from outside and he got in. Carlos was crumbled on the floor, half conscious. In his hand was a bottle half empty of prescription pills. They were sleeping pills, Edelbert rushed in the bathroom and took over from dad.

"It is a good thing we have got a doctor here," dad said with a sigh of relief.

Edelbert tried to get Carlos to vomit, but he was too weak to do so.

"Call the ambulance!" he said to Sophia who was by the doorway.

While Sophia went to call for an ambulance, Edelbert was trying to keep Carlos conscious. He splashed cold water on his face, and kept talking to him. Eventually Carlos came round, and Edelbert managed to get him to vomit. By the time the ambulance arrived Carlos was looking much better. They had to take him to hospital anyway, just to check him out and see the level of the damage and give him further treatment. He stayed in hospital overnight and was discharged following morning. Dad picked him up from the hospital. He started claiming to seeing Audrey.

"She is coming for me!, and along with others!," he shouted hysterically.

"What others?" asked dad.

"I don't know, but I know they are coming," said Carlos nervously.

"Get them away from me! I don't know where the book is!" he screamed.

"There is Audrey there, and the others, can't you see them," he asked.

"We can't see a thing Carlos, I think you are hallucinating," replied dad.

Mum eventually managed to calm him down, she always had her way with him. Before long father Dowling turned up. None of us wanted to see him, but dad decided to be polite and answered the door.

"How is Carlos?" he asked.

"I am sure he has got a lot to say to you," father Dowling continued.

"What is he talking about?" I whispered to Charlotte. Carlos was dosing away on the settee in the drawing room. "There is something I want to show you," father Dowling told dad.

He led dad upstairs to Charlotte's room, and stood by the fireplace.

"This is where it is," he chuckled.

"What are we supposed to be looking for. And here is what?" dad questioned.

"The original black book is in there," he said while pointing up the chimney.

"Carlos told me everything. I talked him into confession about what he knows and his involvement with the cult. He is somewhat of a con artist, your Carlos," he added.

"I don't believe you," replied dad.

Father Dowling peered up the chimney, and started feeling the inside corners of the fire funnel. He felt something.

"I have got it, here it is," he cried. "Come feel it yourself," he insisted.

Dad crept halfway inside the fireplace, he felt the box which was attached to the inside of the chimney wall. He shook the box trying to yank it off the wall, eventually he succeeded. The box was locked and it was inscribed SAC. Dad and father Dowling brought the box downstairs, where we all felt puzzled by the findings.

"SAC, how was the locked box related to something that I had seen before?" I questioned.

Of cause it was the key that Charlotte and I had found inside that air vent in her bedroom. The whole family was now so familiar with the SAC inscriptions. They were everywhere, from the two black books that we came across, to the key and of cause dad's dream.

"Where is that black key that we found?" I questioned Charlotte.

It was in her chest of drawers, she had tucked it away safely underneath her clothes. We got the key and opened the box. Inside the box was a big black book that resembled the one that we had gotten from Carlos' cottage.

"That's the one!" father Dowling said.

I couldn't believe we trusted Carlos. To think all this while he was fooling us, and even to go as far as sacrificing Audrey to some cult. It was difficult for the whole family, even Edelbert was dumb founded.

Carlos was beginning to stir, we didn't know whether to confront him about the book, or simply hide it from him, till we figured out what to do next.

"Ring father Francis," father Dowling suggested.

"I know everything that has been happening here, that is why I volunteered to take over from vicar Simms," he added.

"I know father Francis isn't well, but the grace of God and faith will bring him here, so that we end this thing," he concluded.

Dad followed suit, he rang the vicarage, father Francis had started recovering. He was talking and barely he could walk. It was a big improvement from when we last saw him. He came to the phone, his voice was slurred because when he gained consciousness, he had suffered a silent stroke.

Carlos had no idea about what was going on, till father Francis turned up. He turned up in a taxi, he could barely walk. He had managed to sneak away from the nuns who were meant to be looking after him at the vicarage. He brought his holy bible, and another bible for ritual exorcisms. With him, he had a few silver coins like he had before, and a few rossary beads. Father Dowling greeted him on his arrival.

"We have got no time to waste, we have got to begin soon," he said.

He looked extremely pale as if he was on death's door. His speech was slurred and his whole deminour appeared lost and confused.

"Where is Carlos? He has got to be there when we do the final ritual, or else it won't work," he insisted.

"What is it we have got to do father?" father Dowling questened.

"We need to go to the Abbey, take the black book with us, and do everything that we did in the previous exorcism. We have got to burn that book at the alter," he said.

We all gathered to go to the abbey, we shared two cars between us. Carlos was in oblivion to what was going on, he just followed blindly till we arrived at the abbey, that is when he started suspecting.

Father Francis started the ritual, calle upon the spirits of father Santos and the others at the alter. Fire broke out at the alter, and before long the abbey was restored to its old self. There was candles lit everywhere, it was no longer a ruin, but a procession was happening, conducted by father Santos. There was dozens of familys who had perished in fire at Bramwells, resurrected. Mr Adamsons was there, and many others, including Audrey and the electrian.

"You have come to join us as our bible prophicies! Mr Thomson! You are one of us, and you have always been!" Adamson cried out.

"Not today! not as long as I live!" father Francis shouted. "Give me the book!" he ordered father Dowling.

Father Dowling handed him the book. After intense prayers and latin chntings, he threw the book in the fire, alongside the silver coins, and rosary beads. There was loud screams coming out of the fire. By then we all held our hands in circle.

"Do not break the circle!" father Francis shouted. "I can't betray them!" Carlos shouted.

He broke the circle, and jumped in the fire, where he perished. Now a gap had been formed that broke the circle, dad got absorbed in the fire, and so was mum. They were holding Carlos' hands before he broke the circle. After them was father Francis, Sophia, and Charlotte who got consumed in the fires. Lucky enough for me and Edelbert, father Dowling yelled out to us to run from the semi circle. We did that, and he saved us. It was now about the aftermath, my family was gone, father Francis and Carlos as well.

The three of felt relief, when it was all over, and yet great sorrow that it did it not turn out the way that we had hoped for. Our faces were covered in ash, and we sat by the stairway of the old abbey ruin. I couldn't think about what had just happened, I was too exhausted. Father Dowling comforted Edelbert and I, and we did not speak much while sat on those stairs. Acouple of hours or more passed, that is when we stood up, after moments of recovery.

"What are you going to do now?" father Dowling asked me.

"You can always stay at mine's for a few days till you figure out about what you are going to do," he said. His hand was around my shoulders, I immediately hugged him.

"Thank you," I said, "let me think about it I replied.

He shook Edelberts hand and then he left us. We watched him drive off the abbey ruins, till his car lost visibility behind the abbey bushes. Now it was just Edelbert and I, we did not want to talk about what had just happened, we had to reserve that for another time, and another era.

"Are you going to come with me then?" he asked softly. I gave him a hug, and thanked him for everything.

"I don't think so," I replied. "I guess, I have got to find out things myself now," I smiled.

He drove off, and left me there wondering at the abbey ruins, trying to figure out what had just gone on. From then on, I was going to book into a hotel, and the rest was unknown.